BA ☑ S0-AXY-370

is a pulse-racing mixture of laughter and thrills as only Donald E. Westlake, the undisputed master of comic suspense, can provide.

"Westlake is the Mario Puzo of disorganized crime...and BANK SHOT goes right into the same happy pocket as THE HOT ROCK."
—Ira Levin, author of *Rosemary's Baby*

"Gorgeously complicated...another don't-miss item from Westlake."
—*San Francisco Examiner and Chronicle*

"...Westlake is a writer of uncommon talent, imagination, flair, and unpredictability."
—Richard S. Lochte II, *Los Angeles Times*

"A choice assortment of oddballs...the plot is a beauty, and the ending is unbelievable.... Try it, you'll like it."   —Associated Press

Debbie

BANK SHOT
was originally published by Simon and Schuster.

BANK
SHOT

Donald E. Westlake

PUBLISHED BY POCKET BOOKS NEW YORK

BANK SHOT

Simon and Schuster edition published 1972

POCKET BOOK edition published May, 1973

5th printing..........................July, 1974

L

Standard Book Number: 671-77643-6.
Library of Congress Catalog Card Number: 72-183763.
This POCKET BOOK edition is published by arrangement with Simon & Schuster, Inc. Copyright, ©, 1972, by Donald E. Westlake.

Printed in the U.S.A.

For BILL GOLDMAN
Here's something to think about at the icebox.

BANK
SHOT

1

"YES," Dortmunder said. "You can reserve all this, for yourself and your family, for simply a ten-dollar deposit."

"My," said the lady. She was a pretty woman in her mid-thirties, small and compact, and from the looks of this living room she kept a tight ship. The room was cool and comfortable and neat, packaged with no individuality but a great passion for cleanliness, like a new mobile home. The draperies flanking the picture window were so straight, each fold so perfectly rounded and smooth, that they didn't look like cloth at all but a clever plaster forgery. The picture they framed showed a neat treeless lawn that drained away from the house, the neat curving blacktop suburban street in spring sunshine, and a ranch-style house across the way identical in every exterior detail to this one. *I bet their drapes aren't this neat,* Dortmunder thought.

"Yes," he said, and gestured at the promo leaflets now scattered all over the coffee table and the nearby floor. "You get the encyclopedia *and* the bookcase *and* the Junior Wonder Science Library and *its* bookcase, *and* the globe, and the five-year free use of research facilities at our gigantic modern research facility at Butte, Montana, and—"

"We wouldn't have to *go* to Butte, Montana, would we?" She was one of those neat, snug women who can still look pretty with their brows furrowed. Her true role in life would be to operate a USO canteen, but here she was in this white-collar ghetto in the middle of Long Island.

"No, no," Dortmunder said with an honest smile. Most of the housewives he met in the course of business left him cold, but every once in a while he ran across one like this who hadn't been lobotomized by life in the suburbs, and the contact always made him cheerful. *She's sprightly,* he thought, and smiled some more at the rare chance to use a word like that, even in interior monologue. Then he turned the smile on the customer and said, "You *write* to them in Butte, Montana. You tell them you want to know about, uh . . ."

"Anguilla," she suggested.

"Sure," Dortmunder said, as though he knew just what she meant. "Anything you want. And they send you the whole story."

"My," she said and looked again at all the promo papers spread around her neat living room.

"And don't forget the five annual roundups," Dortmunder told her, "to keep your encyclopedia right up to date for the next five years."

"My," she said.

"And you can reserve the whole thing," Dortmunder said, "for a simple ten-dollar deposit." There had been a time when he had been using the phrase "measly ten-dollar deposit," but gradually he'd noticed that the prospects who eventually turned the deal down almost always gave a visible wince at the word "measly," so he'd switched to "simple" and the results had been a lot better. Keep it simple, he decided, and you can't go wrong.

"Well, that's certainly something," the woman said. "Do you mind waiting while I get my purse?"

"Not at all," Dortmunder said.

She left the room, and Dortmunder sat back on the sofa and smiled lazily at the world outside the picture window. A man had to stay alive somehow while waiting for a big score to develop, and there was nothing better for that than an encyclopedia con. In the spring and fall, that is; winter was too cold for house-to-house work and summer was too hot. But given the right time of year, the old encyclopedia scam was unbeatable. It kept you in the fresh air and in nice neighborhoods, it gave you a chance to stretch your legs in comfortable living rooms and chat with mostly pleasant suburban ladies, and it bought the groceries.

Figure ten or fifteen minutes per prospect, though the losers usually didn't take that long. If only one out of five bit, that was ten bucks an hour. On a six-hour day and a five-day week, that was three hundred a week, which was more than enough for a man of simple tastes to live on, even in New York.

And the ten-dollar bite was just the perfect size. Anything smaller than that, the effort wouldn't be worth the return. And if you went up above ten dollars, you got into the area where the housewives either wanted to talk it over with their husbands first or wanted to write you checks; and Dortmunder wasn't about to go cash a check made out to an encyclopedia company. The few checks he got at the ten-dollar level he simply threw away at the end of the day's business.

It was now nearly four in the afternoon. He figured he'd make this the last customer of the day, go find the nearest Long Island Railroad station, and head on back into the city. May would be home from Bohack's by the time he got there.

Should he start packing the promo material back in his attaché case? No, there wasn't any hurry. Besides, it was psychologically good to keep the pretty pictures out where the customer could see what she was buying until she'd actually handed over the ten spot.

Except that what she was really buying with her ten dollars was a receipt. Which he might as well get out, come to think of it. He opened the snaps on the attaché case beside him on the sofa and lifted the lid.

To the left of the sofa was an end table holding a lamp and a cream-colored European-style telephone, not normal Bell issue. Now, as Dortmunder reached into his attaché case for his receipt pad, this telephone said, very softly, "dit-dit-dit-dit-dit-dit-dit-dit-dit."

Dortmunder glanced at it. His left hand was holding the lid of the case up, his right hand was inside holding the receipt pad, but he didn't move. Somebody must be dialing an extension somewhere else in the house. Dortmunder frowned at the phone and it said, "dit." A smaller number that time, probably a 1. Then "dit," said the phone again, which would be another 1. Dortmunder waited, not moving, but the phone didn't say anything else.

Just a three-digit number? A high digit first, and then two low ones. What kind of phone number was . . .

911. The police emergency number.

Dortmunder took his hand out of the attaché case without the receipt pad. No time to pick up the promo papers. He methodically snicked shut the attaché case snaps, got to his feet, walked to the door, opened it, and stepped outside. Carefully closing the door behind him, he walked briskly over the curving slate path to the sidewalk, turned right, and kept on walking.

What he needed was a store, a movie theater, a cab, even a church. Someplace to get inside for a little while. Walking along the street like this, he didn't have a chance. But there was nothing as far as the eye could see, nothing but houses and lawns and tricycles. Like the Arab who fell off his camel in *Lawrence of Arabia,* Dortmunder just kept walking, even though he was doomed.

A purple Oldsmobile Toronado with MD plates roared by, heading in the direction he was coming from. Dortmunder thought nothing of it until he heard the brakes squeal back there, and then his face lit up and he said, "Kelp!"

He turned to look, and the Oldsmobile was making a complicated U-turn, backing and filling, making little progress. The driver could be seen spinning the wheel madly, first in one direction and then the other, like a pirate captain in a hurricane, while the Oldsmobile bumped back and forth between the curbs.

"Come *on,* Kelp," Dortmunder muttered. He shook the attaché case a little, as though to help straighten the car out.

Finally the driver lunged the car up over the curb and in a sweeping arc over the sidewalk and back down, and slammed it to a stop in front of where Dortmunder was standing. Dortmunder, whose enthusiasm had already faded somewhat, opened the passenger door and slid in.

"So there you are," Kelp said.

"There I am," Dortmunder said. "Let's get out of here."

Kelp was aggrieved. "I been looking all over for you."

"You aren't the only one," Dortmunder said. He twisted around to look out the rear window; nothing yet. "Come on, let's go," he said.

But Kelp was still aggrieved. "Last night," he said, "you told me you were gonna be today in Ranch Cove Estates."

Dortmunder's attention had been caught. "I'm not?"

Kelp pointed at the windshield. "Ranch Cove Estates stops three blocks down there," he said. "This is Elm Valley Heights."

Dortmunder looked around at no elms, no valleys and no heights. "I must have slipped across the border," he said.

"I been driving up and down and up and down. I just now gave up, I was going back to the city, I figured I never would find you."

Was that a siren in the distance? "Well, now you found me," Dortmunder said. "So why don't we go someplace?"

But Kelp didn't want to distract himself with driving. He had the engine still running, but the gear shift was in *Park* and he had more to say. "Do you know what it's like, you spend the whole day just driving up and down and up and down, and the guy you're looking for isn't even *in* Ranch Cove Estates?"

It was definitely a siren, and it was coming closer. Dortmunder said, "Why don't we go there now?"

"Very funny," Kelp said. "Do you realize I had to put a dollar's worth of gas of my own money in this car, and it was almost full when I picked it up?"

"I'll reimburse you," Dortmunder said. "If you'll just use some of it to drive us away from here." Far down the street was a tiny winking red light, and it was coming this way.

"I don't want your money," Kelp said. He was somewhat mollified, but still irritated. "All I want is if you say you're gonna be in Ranch Cove Estates *be* in Ranch Cove Estates."

There was a police car under the winking red light, and it was coming like hell. "I'm sorry," Dortmunder said. "From now on I'll do better."

Kelp frowned at him. "What? That's not like you, to talk like that. Something wrong?"

The police car was two blocks away and moving fast. Dortmunder put his head in his hands.

Kelp said, "Hey, what's the matter?" He said something else after that, but the noise of the siren was so loud that his voice was blotted out. The siren shrilled to a peak of noise, and then modulated all at once into minor key and receded.

Dortmunder lifted his head and looked around. The police car was a block behind them and slowing at last as it neared the house Dortmunder had come from.

Kelp was frowning at the rear-view mirror. "I wonder who they want," he said.

"Me," Dortmunder said. His voice was a little shaky. "Now do you mind if we go away from here?"

2

KELP drove along with one eye on the empty street ahead and one eye on the rear-view mirror showing the empty street behind. He was tense but alert. He said, "You should've told me sooner."

"I tried," Dortmunder said. He was being sullen and grumpy in the corner,

"You could've got us both in trouble," Kelp said. The

memory of the police car's siren was making him nervous, and nervousness made him talkative.

Dortmunder didn't say anything. Kelp took a quick glance at him and saw him brooding at the glove compartment, as though wondering if it had an ax in it. Kelp went back to watching the street and the rear-view mirror and said, "With that record of yours, you know, you get picked up for anything, you'll get life."

"Is that right?" Dortmunder said. He was really being very sour, even worse than usual.

Kelp drove one-handed for a minute while he got out his pack of Trues, shook one out, and put it between his lips. He extended the pack sideways, saying, "Cigarette?"

"True? What the hell kind of brand is that?"

"It's one of the new ones with the low nicotine and tars. Try it."

"I'll stick to Camels," Dortmunder said, and out of the corner of his eye Kelp saw him pull a battered pack of them from his jacket pocket. "True," Dortmunder grumbled. "I don't know what the hell kind of name that is for a cigarette."

Kelp was stung. He said, "Well, what kind of name is Camel? True *means* something. What the hell does Camel mean?"

"It means cigarettes," Dortmunder said. "For years and years it means cigarettes. I see something called True, I figure right away it's a fake."

"Just because you've been working a con," Kelp said, "you figure everybody else is too."

"That's right," Dortmunder said.

Kelp could deal with anything at that point except being agreed with; not knowing where to go from there, he let the conversation lapse. Also, realizing he was still holding the cigarette pack in his right hand, he tucked it away again in his shirt pocket.

Dortmunder said, "I thought you quit anyway."

Kelp shrugged. "I started again." He put both hands on the wheel while he negotiated a right turn onto Merrick Avenue, a major street with a good amount of traffic.

Dortmunder said, "I thought the cancer commercials on television scared you off."

"They did," Kelp said. There were now cars both in front of him and behind him, but none of them contained police. "They don't show them any more," he said. "They took the cigarette commercials off, and they took the cancer commercials off at the same time. So I went back." Still watching the street, he reached out to press the lighter button in. Windshield washer fluid suddenly sprayed all over the glass in front of him, and he couldn't see a thing.

Dortmunder shouted, "What the hell are you doing?"

"God *damn* it!" Kelp yelled and stomped on the brake. It was a power brake, and the car stopped on a dime and gave them change. "These American cars!" Kelp yelled, and something crashed into them from behind.

Dortmunder, peeling himself off the dashboard, said, "I suppose this is better than life imprisonment."

Kelp had found the windshield wipers and now they started sweeping back and forth over the glass, flinging gobs of fluid left and right. "We're okay now," Kelp said, and somebody knocked on the side window next to his left ear. He turned his head, and there was a heavyset guy in a topcoat out there, shouting. "Now what?" Kelp said. He found the button that would slide the power window down, pushed it, and the power window slid down. Now he could hear that the heavyset guy was shouting, "Look what you done to my car!"

Kelp looked out front, but there wasn't anything in front of him at all. Then he looked in the rear-view mirror and saw a car very close to him in the back.

The heavyset guy was shouting, "Come look! Come see for yourself!"

Kelp opened the car door and got out. A bronze Pinto was nuzzling the purple Toronado in the rear. Kelp said, "Well, for Christ's sake."

"Look what you done to my car!"

Kelp walked down to where the two cars met and studied the damage. Glass was broken, chrome was bent, and what looked like radiator fluid was making a green puddle on the blacktop.

"I tell you," the heavyset guy shouted, "to go ahead, just go ahead and look what you done to my car!"

Kelp shook his head. "Oh, no," he said. "You hit me from the rear. I didn't do anything to—"

"You jammed on your brakes! How'm I supposed to—"

"Any insurance company in the world will tell you the driver in the back is the one who—"

"You jammed on your— We'll see what the cops say!"

The cops. Kelp gave the heavyset guy a bland, unworried smile and started to walk around the Pinto, as though to inspect the damage on the other side. There was a row of stores on the right here, and he'd already spotted an alley between two of them.

On the way around the Pinto, Kelp glanced in and saw that the storage area in back was full of open-top cardboard cartons full of paperback books. About five or six titles, with dozens of copies of each title. One was called *Passion Doll,* another *Man Hungry,* another *Strange Affair.* The covers featured undressed girls. There were *Call Me Sinner* and *Off Limits* and *Apprentice Virgin.* Kelp paused.

The heavyset guy had been following him, ranting and raving, waving his arms around so that his topcoat flapped —imagine somebody wearing a topcoat on a day like this—but now he stopped when Kelp did, and his voice lowered, and in an almost normal tone of voice he said, "So what?"

Kelp stood looking in at the paperback books. "You were talking about the cops," he said.

Other traffic was now having to detour around them. A woman in a Cadillac shouted as she went by, "Why don't you bums get off the road?"

"I'm talking about *traffic* cops," the heavyset guy said.

"Whatever you're talking about," Kelp said, "what you're gonna get is cops. And they're likely to care more about the back of your car than the front."

"The Supreme Court—"

"I didn't figure we'd get the Supreme Court to come out for a traffic accident," Kelp said. "What I figured, we'd probably get just local Suffolk County cops."

"I got a lawyer to handle that," the heavyset guy said, but he didn't seem as sure of himself any more.

"Also, you hit me from behind," Kelp said. "Let's not leave that out of our calculations."

The heavyset guy looked quickly all around, as though for an exit, and then looked at his watch. "I'm late for an appointment," he said.

"So am I," said Kelp. "What I figure, what the hell, we've got the same amount of damage on each car. I'll pay for mine, you pay for yours. We put a claim in with the insurance company, they'll just up our rates."

"Or drop us," the heavyset guy said. "That happened to me once already. If it wasn't for a guy my brother-in-law knew, I wouldn't have insurance right now."

"I know how it is," Kelp said.

"Those bastards'll rob you deaf, dumb and blind," the heavyset guy said, "and then all of a sudden *boom*—they drop you."

"We're better off we don't have anything to do with them," Kelp said.

"Fine by me," the heavyset guy said.

"Well, I'll see you around," Kelp said.

"So long," said the heavyset guy, but even as he said it he was starting to look puzzled, as though beginning to suspect he'd missed a station somewhere along the way.

Dortmunder wasn't in the car. Kelp shook his head as he put the Toronado in drive. "Oh, ye of little faith," he said under his breath and drove off with a grinding of metal.

He didn't realize he'd carried the Pinto's front bumper away with him until two blocks later, when he started up from a traffic light and it fell off back there with one hell of a crash.

3

DORTMUNDER had walked three blocks along Merrick Avenue, swinging his almost-empty attaché case, when the purple Toronado pulled to the curb beside him again and Kelp shouted, "Hey, Dortmunder! Get in!"

Dortmunder leaned down to look through the open right-side window. "I'll take the train," he said. "Thanks, anyway." He straightened and walked on.

The Toronado shot past him, went down a line of parked cars and pulled in by a fire hydrant. Kelp jumped out, ran around the car and met Dortmunder on the sidewalk. "Listen," he said.

"Things have been very quiet," Dortmunder told him. "I want to keep it that way."

"Is it my fault that guy ran into me in the back?"

"Have you seen the back of that car?" Dortmunder asked him. He nodded at the Toronado, which he was even then walking past.

Kelp fell into step beside him. "What do I care?" he said. "It's not mine."

"It's a mess," Dortmunder said.

"Listen," Kelp said. "Don't you want to know what I was looking for you for?"

"No," Dortmunder said. He kept walking.

"Where the hell you walking to anyway?"

"That railroad station down there."

"I'll drive you."

"You sure will," Dortmunder said. He kept walking.

"Listen," Kelp said. "You've been waiting for a big one, am I right?"

"Not again," Dortmunder said.

"Will you listen? You don't want to spend the rest of your life pedding encyclopedias around the Eastern Seaboard, do you?"

Dortmunder said nothing. He kept walking.

"Well, do you?"

Dortmunder kept walking.

"Dortmunder," Kelp said, "I swear and vow I have the goods. This time I have a guaranteed winner. A score so big you can retire for maybe three years. Maybe even four."

"The last time you came to me with a score," Dortmunder said, "it took five jobs to get it, and even when I got it I didn't have anything." He kept walking.

"Is that my fault? Luck ran against us, that's all. The idea of the caper was first-rate, you got to admit that yourself. Will you for Christ's sake stop walking?"

Dortmunder kept walking.

Kelp ran around in front of him and trotted backward for a while. "All I'm asking," he said, "is that you listen to it and come look at it. You know I trust your judgment; if you say it's no good I won't argue for a minute."

"You're gonna fall over that Pekingese," Dortmunder said.

Kelp stopped running backward, turned around, glared back at the woman who owned the Pekingese, and reverted to walking frontward, on Dortmunder's left. "I think we been friends long enough," he said, "that I can ask you as a personal favor just to give me a listen, just to give the job a look-see."

Dortmunder stopped on the sidewalk and gave Kelp a heavy look. "We been friends long enough," he said, "that I know if you come up with a job, there's something wrong with it."

"That isn't fair."

"I never said it was."

Dortmunder was about to start walking again when Kelp quickly said, "Anyway, it isn't my caper. You know about my nephew Victor?"

"No."

"The ex-FBI man? I never told you about him?"

Dortmunder looked at him. "You have a nephew who's an FBI man?"

"*Ex*-FBI man. He quit."

"He quit," Dortmunder echoed.

"Or maybe they fired him," Kelp said. "It was some argument about a secret handshake."

"Kelp, I'm gonna miss my train."

"I'm not making this up," Kelp said. "Don't blame me, for Christ's sake. Victor kept sending in these memos how the FBI ought to have a secret handshake, so the agents could tell each other at parties and like that, and they never went for it. So either he quit or they fired him, something like that."

"This is the guy that came up with the caper?"

"Look, he was *in* the FBI, he passed the tests and everything, he isn't a nut. He's got a college education and everything."

"But he wanted them to have a secret handshake."

"Nobody's perfect," Kelp said reasonably. "Hey, listen, will you come meet him, listen to him? You'll like Victor. He's a nice guy. And I tell you the score is guaranteed beautiful."

"May's waiting for me to come home," Dortmunder said. He could feel himself weakening.

"I'll give you the dime," Kelp said. "Come on, whadaya say?"

"I'm making a mistake," Dortmunder said, "that's what I say." He turned around and started walking back. After a second, Kelp caught up with him again, smiling cheerfully, and they walked back together.

The Toronado had a ticket on it.

4

"EVERYBODY FREEZE," Victor snarled. "This is a stickup."

He pushed the stop button on the cassette recorder, rewound, and played it back. "Everybody freeze," the cassette snarled. "This is a stickup."

Victor smiled, put the recorder down on his work table, and picked up both other recorders. All three were small, about the size of a tourist's camera. Into one of them Victor said, in a high-pitched voice, "You can't do this!" Then he played that from one recorder into the other, at the same time giving a falsetto "Eeek!" The scream and the high-pitched remark were then played back from recorder number three to recorder number two, while in a deep voice Victor said, "Look out, boys, they've got guns!" Gradually, working back and forth between the recorders, he built up an agitated crowd response to the stickup announcement, and when he was satisfied with it he recorded it onto the first cassette.

The room Victor was in had started life as a garage but had veered. It was now a cross between a den and a radio repair shop, plus some Batcave. Victor's work table, littered with recording equipment, old magazines and odds and ends, was against the rear wall, which was completely papered with covers from old pulp magazines, pasted on and then shellacked. At the top of the wall was a rolled-up motion-picture screen, which could be pulled down and hooked to a gizmo at the back of the work table.

The wall to Victor's left was lined with bookcases, filled with pulp magazines, paperback books, Big Little Books, comic books, and elderly hardcover boys' books—Dave

Dawson, Bomba, the Boy Allies. The wall to his right was also lined with shelves, these containing stereo components and records, mostly old sixteen-inch transcription records of radio shows like "The Lone Ranger" and "Terry and the Pirates." On a small shelf at the bottom were a line of new cassettes, identified in neat lettering in red ink with such titles as *The Scarlet Avenger Meets Lynxman* and *"Rat" Duffy's Mob Breaks Out.*

The last wall, where the garage doors had once been, was now given over to motion pictures. There were two projectors, an eight-millimeter and a sixteen-, and shelf after shelf of canned film. Stray bits of unused wall around the room sported posters for old movie serials—*Flash Gordon Conquers the Universe*—and box tops from old cereals—Kellogg's Pep, Quaker Puffed Rice, Post Toasties.

There were no doors or windows visible anywhere in the room, and most of the central floor space was taken up by fifteen old movie seats, in three rows of five, all facing the rear wall, the rolled-up screen, the littered work table, and Victor.

Being just thirty years of age, Victor hadn't yet been born when most of the material in the room had first appeared. He'd discovered the pulps by accident when he was in high school, had started collecting, and had gradually spread out to all the sources of adventure in the decades before World War Two. It was history to him, and a hobby, but not nostalgia. His own youth had been highlighted by Howdy Doody and John Cameron Swayze, and he had as yet discovered no twinge of nostalgia within him for either.

Maybe it was his hobby that kept him young. Whatever it was, he didn't look his age. At the most, he might be taken for twenty, but generally the people he met assumed he was a teenager, and he was still routinely asked for proof of age whenever he went into a bar. It had frequently been embarrassing, back when he was with the Bureau, to identify himself to some pinko as an FBI man and have the pinko fall on the floor laughing. His looks had hampered his Bureau activities in other ways, too; for instance, he couldn't infiltrate a college campus because he didn't

look old enough to go to college. Nor could he grow a
beard, except some straggling thing that made him look as
though he was suffering from radiation sickness. And when
he let his hair grow long, the best he could look like was
the Three Musketeers' mascot.

He sometimes thought the reason the Bureau had let
him go was just as much his appearance as the business
about the handshake. Once, when he'd been assigned to
the Omaha office, he'd heard Chief Agent Flanagan say to
Agent Goodwin, "We want our men to look clean-cut, but
that's ridiculous," and he'd known they were talking about
him.

But the Bureau hadn't been the right place for him
anyway. It wasn't anything like *The FBI in Peace and
War,* or *G-Men,* or the rest of the literature. They didn't
even *call* themselves G-men; they called themselves
Agents. Every time he'd called himself "Agent," Victor
had gotten the mental image of himself as an undercover
humanoid from another planet, part of the advance guard
sent to enslave mankind and turn Earth over to the Green
Goks from Alpha Centauri II. It had been a disturbing
mental image and had played havoc with his interrogation
technique.

Also, consider: Victor had been with the Bureau twenty-
three months, and not once had he held in his hands a
submachine gun. He hadn't even *seen* one. He'd never
broken down a door. He'd never held a loud-hailer to his
mouth and bawled, "All right, Muggsy, we've got the
house surrounded." What he'd mostly done was call Army
deserters' parents on the telephone and ask them if they'd
seen their son recently. And he'd also done a lot of filing—
really, one hell of a lot of filing.

No, the Bureau hadn't been the right place for him at
all. But where—other than this garage—was the right place?
He had his law degree, but he'd never taken the bar exam
and had no particular desire to become an attorney. He
made a small living these days as a dealer in old books and
magazines, completely mail order, but it wasn't a really
satisfying existence.

Well, maybe this business with his uncle Kelp would turn out to be something. Time would tell.

"You can't get away with that!" he said in a manly voice into the master cassette, then overlaid a high, squealing, "No, don't!" Then he put down the recorders, opened a drawer of the work table, and took out a small .25-caliber Firearms International automatic. He checked the clip, and it still contained five blanks. Switching on a recorder, he fired two quick shots and then a third, at the same time shouting, "Take that! And that!"

"Uh," said a voice.

Victor turned his head, startled. A section of bookcase in the left-hand wall had opened inward, and Kelp was standing in the doorway, looking glazed. Behind him was a wedge of sunlit back yard and the white clapboard side wall of the neighbor's garage. "I, uh . . ." said Kelp and pointed in various directions.

"Oh, hi," Victor said cheerfully. He waved the gun in friendly fashion and said, "Come on in."

Kelp pointed in the general direction of the gun. "That uh . . ."

"Oh, it's blanks," Victor said easily. He switched off the recorder, put the automatic away in the drawer and got to his feet. "Come on in."

Kelp came in and shut the bookcase. "You don't want to startle me," he said.

"Golly, I'm sorry," Victor said concernedly.

"I startle easy," Kelp said. "You shoot a gun, you throw a knife, any little thing like that will set me right off."

"I'll sure remember that," Victor said soberly.

"Anyway," Kelp said, "I found the guy I was telling you about."

"The planner?" Victor asked with quickening interest. "Dortmunder?"

"That's the one. I wasn't sure you wanted me to bring him in here. I know you like this place kept private."

"That's good," Victor said approvingly. "Where is he?"

"Down the drive."

Victor hurried to the front of the room where the movie

projectors and cans of films were located. A small framed poster for the George Raft *The Glass Key* was at eye level on a clear patch of wall; it was hinged at the top, and Victor lifted it up out of the way and stood close to peer through a small rectangular pane of dusty glass at the world outside.

What he was looking at was the weedy driveway beside his house, with its two narrow ribbons of old cracked concrete leading down to the sidewalk and the street. This was an older section of Long Island than either Ranch Cove Estates or Elm Valley Heights. It was called Belle Vista; the streets were all straight, and the houses ran mostly to two-story, one-family affairs with front porches.

Down at the sidewalk Victor saw a man. He was walking slowly back and forth, he was looking down, and he was taking occasional quick puffs on a stub of cigarette he held in his cupped hand. Victor nodded, pleased at what he saw. Dortmunder was tall and lean and tired-looking; he had the worn look of Humphrey Bogart in *High Sierra*. Victor did a Bogart twitch with the left side of his mouth, leaned back, and lowered the movie poster again. "That's fine," he said amiably. "Let's go out and meet him."

"Sure," Kelp said.

Victor opened the bookcase and bowed Kelp through ahead of him. On the other side, the bookcase was an ordinary door, with a dusty window in it covered by a chintz curtain. Victor pulled the door shut and walked with Kelp around to the front of the garage and down the driveway toward Dortmunder.

Victor couldn't help looking back, when he was halfway down the drive, and admiring his handiwork. From the outside it looked like a perfectly ordinary garage, except that it was more old-fashioned than most, with its pair of side-hinged doors padlocked in the middle. Anybody who went up to those doors and looked through the small dusty windows would see nothing but blackness; it was black felt against plywood six inches from the glass, but he wouldn't know that. He'd think it was simply dark in there. Victor had tried rigging up a blow-up photograph of a 1933 Ford in there, but he just couldn't ever get the perspective right, so he'd settled for darkness instead.

He faced front again, smiling, and walked with Kelp the rest of the way to meet Dortmunder, who stopped on the sidewalk, gave them both a sour look and flicked his cigarette butt away.

Kelp made introductions: "Dortmunder, this is Victor."

"Hello," Dortmunder said.

"Hello, Mr. Dortmunder," Victor said eagerly and stuck his hand out. "I've sure heard a lot about you," he said admiringly.

Dortmunder looked at the hand, then at Victor, and finally shook hands with him, suddenly saying, "You heard a lot about me?"

"From my uncle," Victor said proudly.

Dortmunder gave Kelp a look that wasn't easy to define and said, "Is that right?"

"General things," Kelp said. "You know, just general things."

"This and that," Dortmunder suggested.

"That kind of thing, yeah."

Victor smiled at both of them. Dortmunder was just fine, in appearance and voice and attitude and everything. Just fine. After the disappointment of the Bureau, he hadn't known exactly what to expect, but so far Dortmunder was everything Victor could have hoped for.

He rubbed his hands together in anticipation. "Well," he said happily, "shall we go take a look at it?"

5

THE THREE of them sat in the front seat, with Dortmunder on the right. Every time he turned his head slightly
to the left he saw Victor, sitting in the middle, smiling
at him, as though Victor were a fisherman and Dortmunder was the biggest fish he'd ever caught. It made
Dortmunder very nervous, particularly since this Victor
used to be an FBI man, so he kept his head turned to the
right most of the time and watched the houses go by.
Suburbs, suburbs. All these millions of bedrooms.

After a while Victor said, "Well, we certainly do have
a nice day for it."

Dortmunder turned his head, and Victor was smiling
at him. "Yes," Dortmunder said and turned away again.

"Tell me, Mr. Dortmunder," Victor said, "do you
read newspapers much?"

What kind of question was that? Dortmunder kept his
head turned to the right and mumbled, "Sometimes."

"Any paper in particular?" It was asked in a careless
sort of tone, as though Victor were just making conversation. But it was a weird conversation.

"The *Times* sometimes," Dortmunder said. He watched
an intersection go by.

"That's sort of a liberal paper, isn't it? Is that what
you'd say your politics were? Sort of liberal?"

Dortmunder couldn't help turning and looking at him
again, but Victor was still smiling that same smile, so
Dortmunder quickly looked away again, saying, "Sometimes I read the *News*."

"Ah," said Victor. "I see. Do you find yourself in agree-
ment more often with one paper than the other?"

On Victor's other side, Kelp said, "Lay off, Victor. You quit that job, remember?"

"What? I'm just talking."

"I know what you're just doing," Kelp told him. "But it comes over like a third degree."

"I'm terribly sorry," Victor said. He sounded as though he meant it. "It's just a habit you get into. You'd be surprised how hard it is to break."

Neither Kelp nor Dortmunder commented.

Victor said, "Mr. Dortmunder, I really am sorry. I didn't mean to pry."

Dortmunder sneaked another look at him, and for once he wasn't smiling; he was looking concerned and penitent instead. Dortmunder faced him more securely and said, "That's okay. Think nothing of it."

And Victor smiled again. To the back of Dortmunder's head he said, "I'm sure glad you didn't take offense, Mr. Dortmunder."

Dortmunder grunted, watching houses go by.

"After all, if you don't want to tell me your politics, there's no reason why you should have to."

"Victor," said Kelp warningly.

"What?"

"You're doing it again."

"By golly, so I am. Hey, you're supposed to turn there."

Dortmunder watched the intersection go by and felt the car slowing.

Kelp said, "I'll just make a U-turn."

"Go around the block," Dortmunder said.

"It's just as easy," Kelp said, bringing the car to a stop, "to make a U-turn."

Dortmunder moved his head and gave Kelp a look past Victor's smile. "Go around the block," he said.

Victor, not seeming to notice any tension in the air, pointed out front and said, "Why not just go down there and turn right? Comes out the same place."

"Sure," Kelp said, shrugging, as though it didn't matter one way or the other. The Toronado started forward again, and Dortmunder turned away from Victor's smile once more and watched suburban houses go by. They went through a couple of small shopping areas, each with its own record store and Chinese restaurant, and stopped at last in front of a bank. "There it is," Kelp said.

It was an old-fashioned bank, done in stone that had turned dark gray over the years. Like many banks built in the Northeast in the Twenties, it tried its best to look like a Greek temple, the Twenties being the last decade that Americans actually worshipped money. Like many suburban banks, the Greek-temple motif really wasn't suitable to the size of the building; the four gray stone pillars across the front of it were crammed so close together it was barely possible to get between them to the front door.

Dortmunder spent a few seconds studying that front door, and the pillars, and the sidewalk, and the storefronts on both sides, and then the front door opened and two men in work clothes and construction-crew helmets came out, carrying a tall wooden writing stand, the pens at the end of their chains dangling like remnants of fringe. "We're too late," Dortmunder said.

"Not *that* bank," Kelp said. *"That* bank."

Dortmunder turned his head again, looking at Kelp past Victor's smile. Kelp motioned across the street, and Dortmunder ducked his head a little bit—for one awful second he thought Victor was going to kiss him on the cheek, but he didn't—and looked across the way at the other bank.

At first he didn't see it at all. Blue and white and chrome, something wide and low—that's all he could make out. But then he saw the sign, spread in a banner across the front of the thing:

TEMPORARY   HEADQUARTERS
Capitalists' & Immigrants' Trust
Just Watch Us GROW!

"What the hell is it?" Dortmunder said.

"It's a trailer," Kelp said. "What they call a mobile home. Didn't you ever see that kind of thing before?"

"But what the hell *is* it?"

"It's the bank," Kelp said.

Smiling, Victor said, "They're tearing down the old building, Mr. Dortmunder, and they're going to put the new one up in the same place. So in the meantime they're running the bank from over there in that mobile home."

"In the trailer," Dortmunder said.

"They do that kind of thing all the time," Kelp said. "Didn't you ever notice?"

"I guess so." Dortmunder frowned past their two faces and through the side window and past the traffic and across the opposite sidewalk and tried to make some sense out of what he was looking at, but it was difficult. Particularly with Victor smiling right next to his left ear. "I can't see anything," Dortmunder said. "I'll be right back. You two wait here."

He got out of the Toronado and walked down the block, glancing into the old bank building on the way by. It was nearly five o'clock by now, but the interior was full of men with construction helmets on, ripping things apart in the glare of the work lights. The bank must be in a hell of a hurry to get the old building down and the new one up if they were willing to pay that kind of overtime. Probably nervous about being in the trailer.

At the corner, Dortmunder turned left, waited for the light, and then crossed the street. Turning left again, he strolled along the sidewalk toward the trailer.

It was at the end of the block, in the only vacant lot on the street. It was one of the biggest mobile home units Dortmunder had ever seen, being a good fifty feet long and twelve feet wide. Set back a yard or so from the regular building line, it filled the width of the lot, one end flush against the side of a Kresge five-and-dime and the other end almost reaching the sidewalk on the cross street. The surface of the lot was crushed brick rubble, showing that some other building had also recently been torn down; the bank had probably timed its own reconstruction to the availability of a lot nearby.

There were two entry doors along the front of the trailer, each with a heavy set of temporary wooden steps leading up to it, and the "Temporary Headquarters" sign strung between them. Concrete blocks made a gray foundation wall from the ground up to the bottom edge of the blue and white metal shell, and all the letter-slot-style windows were covered on the inside by venetian blinds. The bank was closed now, but lights could be seen through slits in the blinds.

Dortmunder looked up as he strolled by. A thick sweep of wires connected the trailer to telephone and power poles both on the main avenue and the cross street, as though the trailer were a rectangular dirigible, moored there by all those lines.

There was nothing more to see, and Dortmunder had reached the corner. He waited on the curb for the light again, then crossed the street and went back to the Toronado, shaking his head as he glanced at the rear of the car. He got in and said, "Can't tell much from the outside. You thinking about a day operation or a night operation?"

"Night," Kelp said.

"They leave cash in there overnight?"

"Only on Thursdays." It was Victor who told him that.

Reluctantly, Dortmunder focused on Victor. "How come on Thursdays?"

"Thursday night the stores are open," Victor said. "The bank closes at three, but then opens again at six and stays open till eight-thirty. At that hour of night, there's no simple direct way to get the cash to some other bank. So they lay on more guards and keep the money in the bank overnight."

"How many more guards?"

"A total of seven," Victor said.

"Seven guards." Dortmunder nodded. "What kind of safe?"

"A Mosler. I believe they have it on lease, along with the trailer. It isn't much of a safe."

"We can get into it fast?"

Victor smiled. "Well," he said, "time really isn't a problem."

Dortmunder glanced across the street. "Some of those wires," he said, "are alarms. I figure they're tied into the local precinct."

Victor's smile broadened. Nodding as though Dortmunder had just displayed great brilliance, he said, "That's just what they are. Anything that happens in there after banking hours is recorded down at the police station."

"Which is where?"

Victor pointed straight ahead. "Seven blocks down that way."

"But time isn't a problem," Dortmunder said. "We're going in against seven guards, the precinct is seven blocks away, and time isn't a problem."

Kelp was grinning by now almost as widely as Victor. "That's the beauty of it," he said. "That's the stroke of genius Victor's come up with."

"Tell me," Dortmunder said.

"We steal the bank," Victor said.

Dortmunder looked at him.

Kelp said, "Isn't that a beauty? We don't break *into* the bank, we take the bank away with us. We back up a truck hook onto the bank, and drive it away."

6

WHEN May got home from Bohack's, Dortmunder wasn't there yet. She stood just inside the front door and yelled, "Hey!" twice, and when there wasn't any answer she shrugged and slopped on through the apartment to the kitchen, carrying the two shopping bags of groceries. Being an employee at the supermarket, she in the first place got a cut rate on some items and in the second place could lift other items with no static, so the shopping bags were pretty full. As she once told her friend Betty at the store, another cashier, "I eat all this stuff and it ought to make me fat, but I have to carry it all home, and that keeps me thin."

"You ought to make your husband come get it," Betty had said.

Everybody made the same mistake about Dortmunder being May's husband. She'd never said he was, but on the other hand she never corrected the mistake either. "I like to be thin," she'd said that time and let it go at that.

Putting the two shopping bags down on the kitchen counter now, she became aware of the fact that the corner of her mouth was warm. She was a chain smoker and kept the current cigarette always propped in the left corner of her mouth; when that area got warm, she knew it was time to start a new cigarette.

There was a small callus on the tip of her left thumb, caused by plucking cigarette embers from her lips, but for some reason her fingertips never callused at all. She flipped the half-inch butt from her mouth into the kitchen sink with one practiced wrist movement, and while it sizzled she took the crumpled pack of Virginia Slims from the waist pocket of her green sweater, shook one up, folded the corner of her mouth around the end and went looking for matches. Unlike most chain smokers, she never lit the new one from the old, because the old one was never big enough to hold onto; this meant a continuing problem with matches, similar to the continuing problem of water in some Arab countries.

She spent the next five minutes opening drawers. It was a small apartment—a small living room, a small bedroom, a bathroom so small you'd scrape your knees, a kitchen as big as the landlord's reservation in Heaven—but it was full of drawers, and for five minutes it was full of the swish-thap of drawers being opened and closed.

She found a book of matches at last, in the living room, in the drawer in the table with the television set on it. It was a pretty nice set, in color, not very expensive; Dortmunder had gotten it from a friend who'd picked up a truckload of them. "The funny thing about it," Dortmunder had said when he'd brought the thing home, "all Harry thought he was doing was stealing a truck."

May lit the cigarette and dropped the match in the ashtray next to the TV. She'd been concentrating on nothing but matches for five minutes, but now as her mind cleared she became aware again of the things around her, and the closest was the TV set, so she turned it on. There was a movie just starting. It was in black and white and May preferred to watch things in color since it was a color set, but the movie had Dick Powell in it, so she waited a while. Then it turned out it was called *The Tall Target,* and in it Dick Powell played a New York City policeman named John Kennedy who was trying to stop an assassination attempt on Abraham Lincoln. He was on a train, Dick Powell was, and he kept getting telegrams, so trainmen kept coming down the corridor shouting, "John Kennedy. John Kennedy." This gave May a pleasant feeling of dislocation, so she backed up until her legs hit the sofa bed and sat down.

Dortmunder came home at the most exciting part, of course, and he brought Kelp with him. It was 1860 and Abraham Lincoln was going to his first inauguration, and that's where they wanted to assassinate him. Adolph Menjou was the mastermind of the plot, but Dick Powell—John Kennedy—was too quick for him. Still, it wasn't certain how things would come out.

"I just don't know about Victor," Dortmunder said, but he was talking to Kelp. To May he said, "How you been?"

"Since this morning? On my feet."

"Victor's okay," Kelp said. "Hi, May, how's your back?"

"About the same. It's my legs the last few days. The groceries!"

They both looked at her as she lunged to her feet, the cigarette in the corner of her mouth giving a puff of smoke like a model train as she exhaled. She said, "I forgot to put the groceries away," and hurried for the kitchen, where everything in the shopping bags was wet from the frozen foods defrosting. "Turn up the sound, will you?" she shouted and quickly put things away. In the living room they turned up the sound, but they also talked louder.

Also, the sound was mostly sound effects, with little dialogue. Then a heavy voice that sounded as though it had to be Abraham Lincoln said, "Did ever a President come to his inauguration so like a thief in the night?"

The groceries were away. May walked back into the living room, saying, "Do you suppose he really said that?"

Dortmunder and Kelp had still been talking about somebody named Victor, and now they both turned and looked at her. Dortmunder said, "Who?"

"Him," she said and gestured at the television set, but when they all looked at it the screen was showing a man standing knee deep in water in a giant toilet bowl, spraying something on the under part of the lip and talking about germs. "Not him," she said. "Abraham Lincoln." She felt them both looking at her and shrugged and said, "Forget it." She went over and switched off the set and said to Dortmunder, "How'd it go today?"

"So-so," he said. "I lost my display. I'll have to go get another."

Kelp explained, "Some woman called the cops on him."

May squinted through cigarette smoke. "You getting fresh?"

"Come on, May," Dortmunder said. "You know me better than that."

"You're all alike as far as I can see," she said. They'd met almost a year ago, when she'd caught Dortmunder shoplifting at the store. It was the fact that he hadn't tried any line at all on her, that he hadn't even asked for her sympathy, that had won her sympathy. He'd just stood there, shaking his head, with packages of boiled ham and American cheese falling out of his armpits, and she just hadn't had the heart to turn him in. She still tried to pretend sometimes that he couldn't pierce her toughness, but he could.

"Anyway," Kelp said, "we're none of us gonna have to work that penny-ante stuff for a while."

"I don't know about that," Dortmunder said.

"You're just not used to Victor," Kelp said, "that's the only problem."

"May I never get used to Victor," Dortmunder said.

May dropped backward into the sofa again; she always sat down as though she'd just had a stroke. "What's the story?" she said.

"A bank job," Kelp said.

"Well, yes and no," Dortmunder said. "It's a little more than a bank job."

"It's a bank job," Kelp said.

Dortmunder looked at May as though hoping to find stability and reason there. "The idea is," he said, "if you can believe it, we're supposed to steal the whole bank."

"It's a trailer," Kelp said. "You know, one of those mobile homes? The bank's in there till they put up the new building."

"And the idea," Dortmunder said, "is we hook the bank onto a truck and drive it away."

"Where to?" May asked.

"Just away," Dortmunder said.

"That's one of the things we've got to work out," Kelp said.

"Sounds like you've got a lot to work out," May said.

"Then there's Victor," Dortmunder said.

"My nephew," Kelp explained.

May shook her head. "I never saw a nephew yet," she said, "that was worth his weight in Kiwanis gum."

"Everybody's somebody's nephew," Kelp said.

May said, "I'm not."

"Every man."

"Victor is a weirdo," Dortmunder said.

"But he comes up with good ideas."

"Like secret handshakes."

"He doesn't have to *do* the job with us," Kelp said. "He just pointed to it."

"That's all he has to do."

"He's got all that FBI experience."

May looked alert. "The FBI's after him?"

"He was in the FBI," Kelp said and waved his hand to

indicate he didn't want to explain any more. "It's a long story," he said.

"I don't know," Dortmunder said. He sat down wearily on the sofa beside May. "What I prefer," he said, "is a simple hold-up. You put a handkerchief over your face, you walk in, you show guns, you take the money, you walk away. Simple, straightforward, honest."

"It's getting tougher these days," Kelp said. "Nobody uses money any more. There aren't any payroll jobs because there aren't any payrolls; everybody pays by check. Stores are on credit cards, so they never have any cash either. A bag of money is a very tough thing to find these days."

"Don't I know it," said Dortmunder. "It's all very depressing."

May said to Kelp, "Why don't you go get yourself a beer?"

"Sure. You?"

"Naturally."

"Dortmunder?"

Dortmunder nodded. He was frowning across at the blank television screen.

Kelp went out to the kitchen, and May said, "What do you think of it, really?"

"I think it's the only thing that's come along in a year," Dortmunder said.

"But do you like it?"

"I told you what I liked. I like to go to a shoe factory with four other guys, walk into the payroll office, walk out with the payroll. But everybody pays by check."

"So what are you going to do?"

From the kitchen, Kelp called, "We can get in touch with Murch, have him check it out. He'd be our driver." They could hear him popping can tops out there.

"I got to go with what's there," Dortmunder said, shrugging. Then he shook his head and said, "But I really don't like all this razzle-dazzle. I'm like a regular cowboy and the only place left to work is the rodeo."

"So you look it over," May said, "you see how it pans

out, you don't have to commit yourself one way or the other yet."

Dortmunder gave her a crooked grin. "Keep me out of mischief," he said.

That's what she'd been thinking. She didn't say anything, just grinned back, and was removing a cigarette ember from her mouth when Kelp came in with the beer. "Why don't I do that?" he said, handing the cans around. "Give Murch a call."

Dortmunder shrugged. "Go ahead."

7

STAN MURCH, in a uniform-like blue jacket, stood on the sidewalk in front of the Hilton and watched cab after cab make the loop in to the main entrance. Doesn't anybody travel in their own car any more? Then at last a Chrysler Imperial with Michigan plates came hesitantly up Sixth Avenue, made the left-hand loop into the Hilton driveway and stopped at the entrance. As a woman and several children got out of the doors on the right of the car, toward the hotel entrance, the driver climbed heavily out on the left. He was a big man with a cigar and a camel's-hair coat.

Murch was at the door before it was halfway open, pulling it the rest of the way and saying, "Just leave the keys in it, sir."

"Right," the man said around his cigar. He got out and sort of shook himself inside the coat. Then, as Murch was about to get behind the wheel, the driver said, "Wait."

Murch looked at him. "Sir?"

"Here you go, boy," the man said and pulled a folded dollar bill from his pants pocket and handed it across.

"Thank you, sir," Murch said. He saluted with the hand holding the dollar, climbed behind the wheel, and drove away. He was smiling as he made the right turn into 53rd Street; it wasn't every day a man gave you a tip for stealing his car.

It was rush hour, and several cabs had to be hustled out of their jocks before Murch reached Eleventh Avenue. Three times he got the supreme accolade: Cabbies in his wake opened their doors, put one foot on the pavement, stepped out, and shook their fists.

The West Side Highway was no good at this time of day, as Stan Murch well knew, but it was possible to make fairly good time if one drove *under* it, down along the docks. You had to be willing to go around trucks parked sideways every block or so, but that was all.

The Brooklyn Battery Tunnel was hopeless, as usual, but at rush hour there just isn't any sensible way to get to Brooklyn, so Murch waited it out, revving the engine in *park* and drumming his fingertips on the steering wheel to a stereo cassette of "Mantovani Swings Bartok for Sleepy Lovers"; these cassettes were very nice, particularly in a tunnel where the radio couldn't pick up anything.

On the other side, Murch paid the toll, angled across seven lanes of fist-shakers, and took an obscure exit marked "Local Streets." While the rest of the world faced stop-and-go traffic on Flatbush and Prospect Expressway, Stan Murch angled down through neighborhoods that hadn't seen a strange face since the Brooklyn Navy Yard closed, and in the general vicinity of Sheepshead Bay he stopped in front of a metal garage door in a long gray brick wall and honked three times. A small door beside the garage entrance carried a sign reading "J & L Novelties— Deliveries." This door opened; a thin black man with a sweatband around his head leaned out, and Murch waved at him. The thin man nodded, disappeared, and a second later the metal door began to creak upward.

Murch drove into a huge concrete room that looked much like a parking garage, with metal support pillars spaced all around it. A dozen or so cars were scattered around the walls, leaving most of the space empty. These were all in the process of being repainted. A used oil drum next to one pillar was half full of license plates, most of them from out-of-state. A dozen men, most of them black or Puerto Rican, were working on the cars; this was obviously an equal-opportunity employer. A battered plastic radio in a far corner raspingly played WABC, a local shlock-rock station.

The thin black man with the sweatband motioned for Murch to leave the Imperial over against the wall to the right. Murch left it there, went through the glove compartment on the off chance, found nothing of interest, and walked back over toward the door. The thin man, who had shut the garage door again, grinned at Murch and said, "You sure do bring in a lot of cars."

"The streets are full of them," Murch said. "Tell Mr. Marconi I'd appreciate the money in a hurry, okay?"

"What do you do with all your money?"

"I'm the sole support of my mother."

"She isn't back in the cab yet?"

"Still got the neck brace on," Murch said. "She could drive, but people generally don't like to ride in a cab with a driver with a neck brace on. It's a superstition, I guess."

"How long's she got to keep it on?"

"Till we settle out of court," Murch said. "Tell Mr. Marconi, will you?"

"Sure," the thin man said. "But, by the way, he isn't Mr. Marconi any more. He changed his name to March legally."

"Oh, yeah? How come?"

"The Italian-American Defamation League made him do it."

"Huh," Murch said. He rolled the new name on his lips: "Salvatore March. Doesn't sound bad."

"I don't think he's happy with it, though," said the thin man. "But what's he gonna do?"

"True. See you around."

"So long," said the thin man.

Murch left and walked for blocks before he found a cab. The driver gave him a mournful yet frantic look and said, "Tell me you want to go to Manhattan."

"I'd like to tell you that," Murch said, "but my mother's in Canarsie."

"Canarsie," said the driver. "And I thought it couldn't get worse." He faced front and headed across the sixth and seventh circles of Brooklyn.

After a while, Murch said, "Listen, would you mind a suggestion about the route?"

"Shut your face," said the driver. He said it softly, but he was hunched forward and his hands were gripping the steering wheel very hard.

Murch shrugged. "You're the boss," he said.

They got there eventually. Murch gave him a nearly 15 percent tip, in honor of his mother, and went inside to find his mother walking around without the brace on. "Hey," he said. "What if I was an insurance adjuster?"

"You'd've rung the doorbell," she said.

"Or looked through the window."

"Don't give me a tough time, Stan," she said. "I'm going crazy cooped up in this house."

"Whyn't you go for a walk?"

"I go out with that brace on," she said, "kids come up and want to know am I a publicity stunt for *Beneath the Planet of the Apes*."

"Little bastards," Murch said.

"Language."

"I tell you what. I'll take tomorrow off, we'll go for a ride."

She perked up a bit. "Where to?"

"Montauk Point. Break out the maps. Let's figure a route."

"You're a good boy, Stan," his mother said, and soon the two of them had their heads together over road maps opened on the dining-room table. They were like that when the doorbell rang.

"Damn!" she said.

"I'll get it," Murch said. "You put on your brace."

"I'm using it," she said.

Murch looked at her, and she didn't have it on. "What do you mean, you're using it?"

"You put it upside down on the drainboard," she said, "it's just perfect for drying socks."

"Aw, Mom, you don't take this seriously." The doorbell rang again. "What if that's an insurance adjuster and you've got socks on your neck brace?"

"I'll put it on, I'll put it on," she said, and went away to the kitchen, while Murch moved more slowly toward the front door.

It was Kelp out there. Murch opened the door wide and said, "Hey, come on in. Long time no see."

"I figured I'd—"

"Mom! Forget it!"

Kelp looked a little startled.

Murch said to him, "Sorry, I just didn't want her to put her brace on."

Kelp tried a smile but went on looking baffled anyway. "Sure," he said. "I just figured I'd—"

Murch's Mom appeared with her neck brace on. "You called me?"

"Hey, Mrs. Murch!" said Kelp. "What happened?"

"I wanted to tell you to forget it," Murch said.

"I couldn't make out what you . . ." She stopped and frowned at Kelp. "Kelp?"

"You hurt your neck?"

Disgusted, she said, "I put this thing on for *you?*"

"That's why I called to you," said Murch.

Shaking her head as best she could in the brace, she turned away again, saying, "This thing is cold, and it's wet."

Kelp said, "You put it on for me?"

Murch said, "Well, if you're gonna put socks on it, it's gonna be cold and wet."

"Wait a minute," Kelp said.

"I don't know how much longer I can put up with this," she said and left the room.

Kelp said, "Why don't I go out and walk around the block and then come back?"

Murch looked at him, bewildered. "What for? You feel dizzy or something?"

Kelp glanced around. "No, I guess not. Everything's okay, I guess. I must've come in while there was already a conversation going on."

"Something like that," Murch said.

"I thought so, yeah."

"Well, come on in."

Kelp was already in. He looked at Murch and didn't say anything.

"Oh, yeah," Murch said. He shut the door and said, "We were just in the dining room."

"I'm busting into dinner? Look, I can—"

"No, we were just looking at maps. Come on in."

Murch and Kelp went into the dining room, just as Murch's Mom was coming in from the other direction, patting her shoulders and saying, "It's my cashmere sweater and it's all wet."

Murch said to Kelp, "You wouldn't have something lined up, would you?"

"As a matter of fact, I would. You free to look it over tomorrow?"

"Oh, hell," said Murch's Mom. "There goes our ride out to the Island."

"Out to Long Island?" said Kelp. "That's perfect, that's just what I want, couldn't be better." He approached the table with all its maps. "Is this Long Island? Here, let me show you the exact spot."

"You two talk," Murch's Mom said. "I've got to go change out of this wet sweater before I get a stiff neck."

8

WHEN Dortmunder walked into the O. J. Bar and Grill on Amsterdam Avenue at eight-thirty the next night, there was nobody in the place but three subway motormen, the television set high up on the wall, and Rollo, the bartender. The television set was showing three people scaling a wall, all burdened down with coils of rope and little hammers and walkie-talkies; they were a Negro, a Jew, and a beautiful blond Swedish girl. The three subway motormen, all Puerto Rican, were talking about whether or not there were alligators in the subway tunnels. They were shouting back and forth at the top of their voices, not because they were mad at each other—though they were—but because their jobs had got them used to talking at that volume. "It's in the *sewers* you got the alligators," one of them shouted.

"Them scum tunnels we got, you don't call them sewers?"

"People bring up alligators from Florida," the first one yelled, "little alligators for pets, they get tired of them, they flush them down the toilet. But in the sewer, not in the tunnels. You don't flush toilets into subway tunnels."

"Not much, you don't."

The third one, the gloomiest of them, shouted, "I run over a rat the other day, down by Kingston-Throop, this big." And knocked over his beer.

Dortmunder strolled on down to the end of the bar while Rollo sopped up the spilled beer and drew a new one. The motormen started shouting about other animals that were or weren't in the subway tunnels, and Rollo came heavily along the bar toward Dortmunder. He was a tall, meaty, balding, blue-jawed gent in a dirty white shirt and dirty white apron, and when he reached Dortmunder he said, "Long time no see."

"You know how it is," Dortmunder said. "I been living with a woman."

Rollo nodded sympathetically. "That's death on the bar business," he said. "What you want to do is get married, then you'll start coming out at night."

Dortmunder nodded his head toward the back room. "Anybody there?"

"Your friend, the other bourbon," Rollo said. "Along with a no-proof-of-age ginger ale. They got your glass."

"Thanks."

Dortmunder left the bar and headed for the rear, past the two doors with the dog silhouettes on them and the sign on one door POINTERS and on the other door SETTERS and past the phone booth and through the green door at the back and into a small square room with a concrete floor. None of the walls were visible because practically the whole room was taken up floor to ceiling with beer cases and liquor cases, leaving only a small opening in the middle big enough for a battered old table with a green felt top, half a dozen chairs and one bare bulb with a round tin reflector hanging low over the table on a long black wire.

Kelp and Victor were seated at the table side by side, as though waiting for a big-stakes poker game to start. A bottle of bourbon and a half-empty glass stood in front of Kelp, and a glass with ice cubes and something sparkly and amber stood in front of Victor.

Kelp, cheerful and optimistic, said, "Hi! Murch isn't here yet."

"So I see." Dortmunder sat down in front of the other glass on the table, which was still empty.

"Hello, Mr. Dortmunder."

Dortmunder looked across the table. Victor's smile made him squint, like too much sunlight. "Hello, Victor," he said.

"I'm glad we'll be working together."

Dortmunder's mouth twitched in what might have been

a smile, and he gazed down at his big-knuckled hands on the green felt of the table.

Kelp pushed the bottle toward him. "Have one."

The bottle claimed to be Amsterdam Liquor Store Bourbon—"Our Own Brand." Dortmunder splashed some in his glass, sipped, made a face and said, "Stan's late. That isn't like him."

Kelp said, "While we wait, why don't we work out some of the details on this thing?"

"Just like it was really going to happen," Dortmunder said.

"Of course it's going to happen," Kelp said.

Victor managed to look worried while still smiling. "Don't you think it'll happen, Mr. Dortmunder?"

Kelp said, "Of course it'll happen." To Dortmunder he said, "What about the string?"

Victor said, "String?"

"The crew," Kelp told him. "The group engaged in the operation."

"Oh."

"We don't have the job planned out yet," Dortmunder said.

"What plan?" Kelp asked. "We back up a truck, hook on, drive the thing away. Dump the guards at our leisure, take it someplace else, bust into the safe, go on about our business."

"I think you skipped over a few spots," Dortmunder said.

"Oh, well," Kelp said airily, "there's details to be worked out."

"One or two," Dortmunder said.

"But we have the general outline. And what I figure, we here can handle it, plus Stan to do the driving and a good lockman to get into the safe."

"We here?" Dortmunder asked. He gave Kelp a meaningful look, glanced at Victor, looked back at Kelp again.

Kelp patted the air in a secretive way, hiding it from Victor. "We can talk about all that," he said. "The question now is the lockman. We know we'll need one."

"How about Chefwick? The model-train nut."

Kelp shook his head. "No," he said, "he isn't around any more. He hijacked a subway car to Cuba."

Dortmunder looked at him. "Don't start," he said.

"Start what? I didn't do anything; Chefwick did. He got to run that locomotive in that job with us, and he must've flipped out or something."

"All right," Dortmunder said.

"So he and his wife went to Mexico on vacation, and at Vera Cruz there were these used subway cars that were going on a boat to Cuba, and Chefwick—"

"I said all right."

"Don't blame me," Kelp said. "I'm just telling you what happened." He brightened suddenly, saying, "That reminds me, did you hear what happened to Greenwood?"

"Leave me alone," Dortmunder said.

"He got his own television series."

"I said leave me alone!"

Victor said, "You know someone with his own television series?"

"Sure," Kelp said. "He was on a job with Dortmunder and me one time."

"You wanted to talk about a lockman," Dortmunder said. Somehow his glass was empty. He splashed in some more of the Amsterdam Liquor Store's Own Brand of bourbon.

"I have a suggestion," Kelp said. He sounded doubtful. "He's a good man, but I don't know . . ."

"Who is it?" Dortmunder asked.

"I don't think you know him."

"What's his name?" When dealing with Kelp, Dortmunder just got more and more patient as time went along.

"Herman X."

"Herman X?"

"The only thing," Kelp said, "he's a spade. I don't know if you're prejudiced or not."

"Herman X?"

Victor said primly, "Sounds like a Black Muslim."

"Not exactly," Kelp said. "He's like in an offshoot. I

don't know what they call themselves. His bunch is mad at the people that were mad at the people that were mad at the people that went off with Malcolm X. I think that's right."

Victor frowned into space. "I haven't kept up with that area of subversion," he said. "It wouldn't be the Pan-African Panthers, would it?"

"Doesn't ring a bell."

"The Sons Of Marcus Garvey?"

"No, that's not right."

"The Black Barons?"

"No."

"The Sam Spades?"

Kelp frowned for a second, then shook his head. "No."

"Probably a new splinter," Victor said. "They keep fractionalizing, makes it extremely difficult to maintain proper surveillance. No cooperation at all. I can remember how upset the agents used to get about that."

A little silence fell. Dortmunder sat there holding the glass and looking at Kelp, who was mooning away at the opposite wall. Dortmunder's expression was patient, but not pleased. Eventually, Kelp sighed and shifted and glanced at Dortmunder and then frowned, obviously trying to figure out what Dortmunder was staring at him for. Then all at once he cried, "Oh! The lockman!"

"The lockman," Dortmunder agreed.

"Herman X."

Dortmunder nodded. "That's the one."

"Well," Kelp said, "do you care about him being black?"

Patiently Dortmunder shook his head. He said, "Why should I care about him being black? All I want him to do is open a safe."

"It's just you never know about people," Kelp explained. "Herman says so himself."

Dortmunder poured more bourbon.

"Should I give him a call?"

"Why not?"

Kelp nodded. "I'll give him a call," he said, and the

door opened and Murch came in, followed by his Mom, wearing her neck brace. They were both carrying glasses of beer, and Murch was also carrying a salt shaker. "Hey, Stan!" Kelp said. "Come on in."

"Sorry we're late," Murch said. "Usually, coming back from the Island, I'd take the Northern State and Grand Central and Queens Boulevard to the Fifty-ninth Street Bridge, but figuring the time of day it was, and I was coming uptown—sit down, Mom."

"Victor," Kelp said, "this is Stan Murch, and this is Murch's Mom."

"What happened to your neck, Mrs. Murch?"

"A lawyer," she said. She was in a bad mood.

"So I figured," Murch said, once he and his Mom were both seated, "I'd just stick with Grand Central and take the Triborough Bridge to a hundred and twenty-fifth Street and over to Columbus Avenue and straight down. Only what happened—"

His Mom said, "Can I take this damn thing off anyway in here?"

"Mom, if you'd leave it on you'd get used to it. You take it off all the time, that's why you don't like it."

"Wrong," she said. "I have to put it on all the time. *That's* why I don't like it."

Kelp said, "Well, Stan, did you go take a look at the bank?"

"Let me tell you what happened," Murch said. "Just leave it on, okay, Mom? So we came across Grand Central, and there was a mess this side of La Guardia. Some kind of collision."

"We got there just too late to see it," his Mom said. She was keeping the neck brace on.

"So I had to go along the shoulder and push a cop car out of the way at one point, so I could get off at Thirty-first Street and go down to Jackson Avenue and then Queens Boulevard and the bridge and the regular way after that. So that's why we're late."

"No problem," Kelp said.

"If I'd done my regular route, it wouldn't have happened."

Dortmunder sighed. "You're here now," he said. "That's the important thing. Did you look at the bank?" He wanted to know the worst and get it over with.

Murch's Mom said, "It was a beautiful day for a drive."

"I looked at it," Murch said. He was being very businesslike all of a sudden. "I looked it over very carefully, and I've got some good news and some bad news."

Dortmunder said, "The bad news first."

"No," Kelp said. "The good news first."

"Okay," Murch said. "The good news is it has a trailer hitch."

Dortmunder said, "What's the bad news?"

"It doesn't have any wheels."

"Been nice talking to you," Dortmunder said.

"Wait a minute," said Kelp. "Wait a minute, wait a minute. What do you mean it doesn't have any wheels?"

"Underneath," Murch said.

"But it's a trailer, it's a mobile home. It's got to have wheels."

"What they did," Murch said, "they put it in position, and jacked it up, and took the wheels off. Wheels and axles both."

"But it *had* wheels," Kelp said.

"Oh, sure," Murch said. "Every trailer has wheels."

"So what the hell did they do with them?"

"I don't know. Maybe the company that owns the trailer has them."

Victor suddenly snapped his fingers and said, "Of course! I've seen the same thing at construction sites. They use trailers for field offices, and if it's a long-term job they build foundation walls underneath and remove the wheels."

"What the hell for?" Kelp asked. He sounded affronted.

"Maybe save strain on the tires. Maybe give it more stability."

Murch said, "The point is, it doesn't have wheels."

A little silence fell on the group. Dortmunder, who had just been sitting there letting the conversation wash over him while he basted in his own pessimism, sighed and shook his head and reached for the bourbon bottle again. He knew that May believed that planning even an idiot job that wouldn't ever happen was better than doing nothing at all, and he supposed she was right, but what he wouldn't give for news right now about a factory that still paid cash.

All right. He was the planner—that was his function—so it was up to him to think about the details as they came along. No wheels. He sighed and said to Murch, "The thing is sitting on those concrete block walls, right?"

"That's right," Murch said. "What they must have done, they jacked it up, took the wheels off, put the concrete blocks in place, and lowered the trailer down onto them."

"The concrete blocks are cemented to each other," Dortmunder said. "The question is, are they cemented to the bottom of the trailer?"

Murch shook his head. "Definitely not. The trailer's just resting there."

"With concrete block all around underneath."

"Not on the ends, just along the two sides."

A tiny flicker of interest made Dortmunder frown. "Not at the ends?"

"No," Murch said. "The one end is against the Kresge's next door, and the other end they've just got a wooden lattice across it. So they can get in at it, I guess."

Dortmunder turned his head to look at Victor. For a wonder, Victor wasn't smiling; instead, he was watching Dortmunder with such intensity he looked paralyzed. It wasn't much of an improvement. Squinting, Dortmunder said, "Is there ever any time when the bank is empty? No guards at all?"

"Every night," Victor said. "Except Thursday, when the cash is in it."

"They don't have a night watchman in there?"

"They don't keep any cash there at all," Victor said, "except on Thursdays. Otherwise, there's nothing to steal. And they've got all the normal burglar alarms. And the police patrol the business streets pretty often out there."

"What about weekends?"

"They patrol weekends, too."

"No," Dortmunder said. "What about guards on the weekends? Saturday afternoon, for instance. The thing's empty then?"

"Sure," Victor said. "With so many shoppers going by on Saturday, what do they need with guards?"

"All right," Dortmunder said. He turned back to Murch and said, "Can we get wheels someplace?"

"Sure," Murch said. No hesitation at all.

"You're sure?"

"Absolutely positive. There is totally nothing in the automotive line that I can't get you."

Dortmunder said, "Good. Can we get wheels that will lift the damn thing up off those concrete blocks?"

"We may have to rig something," Murch said. "They've got those walls up pretty high. There may not be any wheels-and-axle combination that big. But we could attach the axle to a kind of platform and then attach the platform to the bottom of the trailer."

"What about jacks?"

Murch shook his head. "What about them?"

"We can get heavy enough jacks to lift that thing?"

"We don't have to," Murch said. "It has its own jacks, four of them, built up into the undercarriage."

Victor said, "Excuse me, Mr. Murch, but how did you—"

"Call me Stan."

"Thank you. I'm Victor. How did you—"

"Hi."

"Hello. How did you find out about the jacks? Did you crawl under the bank and look?"

Murch grinned and said, "Naw. Down in the corner there's the company name that built the thing. Roamerica. Didn't you notice that?"

"I never did," Victor said. He sounded impressed.

"It's a little silver plate near the back," Murch said. "Near Kresge's."

His Mom said, "Stan has a wonderful eye for detail."

"So we went to a place that sells them," Murch said, "and I took a look at the same kind of model."

"With wheels," Kelp said. He was still taking the business of the wheels as a personal insult.

Murch nodded. "With wheels."

"They're really very nice inside," his Mom said. "More roomy than you'd think. I liked the one with the French Provincial motif."

"I like where we live now," Murch said.

"I'm not saying buy one. I just said I liked it. Very clean, very nice. And you know what I thought of that kitchen."

Dortmunder said, "If we got wheels on it, could you drive it away from there?"

Murch's beer was only half gone, but the head was gone entirely. Musing, he shook a little salt into the glass, which restored some head, and passed the shaker to his mom. "Not with a car," he said. "It's too heavy for that. With a truck. The cab of a tractor-trailer—that would be best."

"But it could be done."

"Oh, sure. I'd have to stick to main streets, though. You've got a twelve-foot width. That's pretty wide for going down back roads. Cuts your possibilities for a get-away route."

Dortmunder nodded. "I figured that."

"Also time of day," Murch said. "Late at night would be best, when there's not so much traffic around."

"Well, we'd figure to do it then anyway," Dortmunder said.

"A lot depends," Murch said, "on where you want to take it."

Dortmunder glanced at Kelp, who looked very defensive and said, "We can work that out, we can work it out. Victor and me."

Dortmunder grimaced and looked back at Murch. "Would you be willing to try it?"

"Try what?"

"Driving the bank away."

"Sure! Naturally, that's what I'm here for."

Dortmunder nodded and sat back in his chair. He didn't look specifically at anybody, but brooded at the green felt tabletop. Nobody spoke for half a minute or so, and then Victor said, "Do you think we can do it, Mr. Dortmunder?"

Dortmunder glanced at him, and the intense look was still there. This was originally Victor's notion, of course, so it was only natural he wanted to know if he had a workable idea or not. Dortmunder said, "I don't know yet. It begins to look as though we can take the thing away, but there's still a lot of problems."

Kelp said, "But we can go forward, right?"

Dortmunder said, "You and Victor can look for a place to stash the bank while . . ." He stopped and shook his head. "A place to stash the bank. I can't believe I'm saying a thing like that. Anyway, you two do that, Murch sets up wheels and a truck or whatever, and—"

"There's the question of money," Murch said. "We're gonna need some deep financing on this job."

"That's my department," Kelp said. "I'll take care of that."

"Good," Dortmunder said.

Murch's Mom said, "Is this meeting over? I got to get home and get this brace off."

"We'll be in touch with each other," Dortmunder said.

Kelp said, "You want me to call Herman X?"

Murch said, "Herman X?"

"Sure," Dortmunder said. "Give him a call. But tell him it isn't a definite set-up yet."

Murch said, "Herman X?"

"You know him?" Kelp said. "A lockman, one of the best."

Victor suddenly jumped to his feet and extended his ginger-ale glass over the table. "A toast!" he cried. "One for all and all for one!"

There was a stunned silence, and then Kelp gave a panicky smile and said, "Oh, yeah, sure." He got to his feet with his bourbon glass.

One by one the others also stood. Nobody wanted to

embarrass Victor. They clinked their glasses together over the middle of the table, and again Victor said, loud and clear, "One for all and all for one!"

"One for all and all for one," everybody mumbled.

9

HERMAN X spread black caviar on black bread and handed it across the coffee table to Susan. "I know I have expensive tastes," he said, flashing his frankest smile at his guests, "but the way I think, we pass this way but once."

"Truer words were never spoken," George Lachine said. He and his wife Linda were the token whites at this dinner party, Susan and the other three couples all being black. George was in OEO somewhere—not in fund disbursement, unfortunately—but it was Linda that Herman had his eye on. He still hadn't made up his mind whether he would finish this evening in bed with Linda Lachine or Rastus Sharif, whether he felt tonight straight or gay, and the suspense was delicious. Also the fact that neither of them had shared his bed before, so it would be a new adventure in any case.

Susan gave George an arch look and said, "I know your kind. Grab all you can get." Herman thought it unlikely that Susan really wanted George; she was probably just trying to make Linda angry, since she knew Herman's intentions in that area.

And she was succeeding. While George looked flustered and flattered, Linda gave Susan a tight-lipped look of hate. But she was too cool, Herman noticed, to say anything right now. That pleased him; people being themselves always pleased him. "A dinner party," he had once said, "should be nothing *but* undercurrents."

This one was. Of the ten people present, practically everybody had been to bed at one time or another with everybody else—excluding the Lachines, of course, who were in process of being drawn in right now.

And himself and Rastus. How had he let that fail to happen for so long? Herman glanced over at Rastus now and saw him indolently whispering something to Diane, his long legs stretched out in front of him. Rastus Sharif; he'd chosen the name himself, of course, as representative of the full range of his heritage, both slave and African, and in doing so had made himself a walking insult to practically everybody he met. Black and white alike had trouble bringing themselves to call him "Rastus." Looking at him, Herman thought the delay had probably been caused by his own admiration and envy; how could he go to bed with the only person on earth he didn't feel superior to?

Mrs. Olaffson suddenly appeared in the living-room doorway. "Telephone, sir."

He sat up. "My call from the Coast?" He was aware of the conversations halting around him.

Mrs. Olaffson knew her part: "Yes, sir."

"Be right there." Standing, he said, "Sorry, people, this may take a while. Try to have fun without me."

They made ribald comments in return, and he grinned as he loped from the room. He had given it out that he was employed in "communications," sometimes making it seem as though he meant book publishing and sometimes motion pictures. Vague but glamorous, and no one ever inquired more closely.

Mrs. Olaffson had preceded him to the kitchen, and on the way through he said, "Study door locked?"

"Yes, sir."

"Mind the fort." He patted her pink cheek, went out the apartment's rear door and down the service stairs two at a time.

As usual, Mrs. Olaffson's timing had been perfect. Just as Herman stepped out onto the sidewalk of Central Park West the grimy green-and-white Ford rolled in to the curb by the fire hydrant. Herman pulled the rear door open and slid in beside Van; as he shut the door, Phil, the driver, started the car moving again.

"Here you go," Van said and handed him his mask and gun.

"Thanks," he said and held them in his lap as the Ford headed south toward midtown.

There was no conversation in the car, not even from the fourth man, Jack, who was the newest, on only his second caper. Driving along, Herman looked out the side window and thought about his dinner party, the people there, the way he would spend the latter part of the night, and the menu for dinner.

He had planned the menu with the greatest of care. The cocktails to begin had been Negronis, the power of the gin obscured by the gentleness of vermouth and Campari. The caviar and pitted black olives to nosh on while drinking. Then, at the table, the meal itself would start with black bean soup, followed by poached fillet of black sea bass and a nice bottle of Schwartzekatz. For the entree, a Black Angus steak sauteed in black butter and garnished with black truffles, plus a side dish of black rice, washed down with a good Pinot Noir. For dessert, black-bottom pie and coffee. For after-dinner drinks, a choice of Black Russians or blackberry brandy, with bowls of black walnuts to munch on again in the living room.

Phil pulled to the curb on Seventh Avenue in the upper forties. Herman and Van and Jack got out and walked away around the corner. Ahead of them, the Broadway theater marquees shouldered one another to be seen.

Ahead on the right was the new rock musical *Justice!* It had been panned on the road, it had come into town fully expecting to be a disaster, it had opened last night, and every last New York critic had given it a rave. The line for advance sale tickets had been around the block all day; the producers hadn't expected the cash in-flow and hadn't prepared for it, so the day's receipts were spending the night in the theater safe. Well, part of the night. One of the brothers in the chorus had passed the word to the Movement, and the Movement had quickly assigned Herman and Phil and Van and Jack. They'd met late this afternoon, looked over the brothers' maps of the interior of the theater, worked out their plot, and here they were.

One usher stood in the outer lobby. He was short and stocky and wore a dark-blue uniform. He gave Herman and Van and Jack a supercilious look as they came in through the outer doors and said, "Can I help you?"

"You can turn around," Van said and showed him a gun. "Or I can blow your head off."

"Good *Christ*," the usher said and stepped back into the doors. He also put his hand to his mouth and blanched.

"Now, that's what I call white," Herman said. His own gun remained in his pocket, but he had taken out the mask and was putting it on. It was a simple black mask, the kind the Lone Ranger wears.

"Turn *around*," Van said.

"Better do it," Herman said. "I'm gentle, but he's mean."

The usher turned around. "What do you want? Do you want my wallet? You don't have to hurt me. I won't do any—"

"Oh, be quiet," Van said. "We're all going inside and turn left and go up the stairs. You first. Don't be cute, because we're right behind you."

"I won't be cute. I don't want to be—"

"Just walk," Van said. He gave off such an aura of weary professionalism that his victims almost always fell all over themselves to do what he wanted; not wanting to expose themselves as amateurs to his jaundiced eye.

The usher walked. Van put away his gun and donned his mask. Jack and Herman were already masked, but a casual observer watching them walk across the dark rear of the theater behind the usher wouldn't have realized they had masks on.

A herd of people onstage were shouting a song: "Freedom means I *got* to be, I *got* to be, I *got* to be, Freedom means I *got* to be. Freedom means you *got* to be, you *got* to be . . ."

The stairs were carpeted in dark red and curved to the right. At the top was the loge, and Van poked the usher to make him move to the right, behind the seats and through another door and up a narrow flight of stairs that wasn't carpeted at all.

In the room were six people. Two women and a man were counting money at tables with adding machines. Three men were wearing the uniform of a private protective service, including holstered pistols. Van stuck his foot around the usher's and gave him a shove as they entered the room, so the usher cried out and went sprawling. It distracted everyone long enough for Van and Jack and Herman to line up in a row inside the door, guns in their hands and masks on their faces, establishing that they were already in control.

"Hands up," Van said. "That means you, Grandpa," to one of the guards. "I haven't shot a senior citizen in three months. Don't make me spoil my record."

It sometimes seemed to Herman that Van leaned on people because he *wanted* them to give him an excuse to shoot them, but most of the time he realized that Van was playing a deeper game than that. He leaned hard so people would think he was trying to goad them, so they would think he was a bad-ass killer just barely in control of himself, and the result was that they were always just as nice as pie. Herman didn't know Van's entire history, but he did know there'd never been any shooting on any job the two of them had done together.

Nor would there be on this one. The three guards gave each other sheepish looks and put their hands up, and Jack came around to take their pistols away from them. Van produced two shopping bags from under his jacket, and while he held a gun on the seven civilians in the room—the usher had come up holding his nose, but it wasn't bleeding—Herman and Jack dumped cash money into the two bags. They put crumpled paper on top, and Herman glanced almost longingly at the safe in the corner. He was a lockman—that was his specialty—he could open safes better than Jimmy Valentine. But this safe was already standing open, and there was nothing in it of any value anyway. He was along simply as a yegg this time, part of the team.

Well, it was for the Cause. Still, it would have been nice if there'd been a safe around to open.

Using the victims' ties and socks and shoelaces and belts, all seven were quickly tied up and left in a neat row on the floor. Then Jack unscrewed the phone from its connection on the wall.

Van said, "What the hell you doing? Just yank the cord out of the wall. Didn't you ever see any movies?"

"I need an extension in the bedroom," Jack said. He put the phone on top of the crumpled papers in one of the shopping bags.

Van shook his head, but didn't say anything.

When they left, they locked the door behind themselves and trotted down the narrow stairs to pause for a second behind the door leading to the loge. They could hear the chorus ripping through another song: "I hate bigots! Dig it! Dig it!"

"The line we're waiting for," Van said, "is 'Love everybody, you bastards.'"

Herman nodded, and all three listened some more. When the line sounded, they pushed the door open, walked through, turned left and headed back downstairs.

The timing was perfect. As they came to the foot of the stairs the curtain came down on Act One, and people started up the aisle for a smoke break. The three men pulled their masks off and went through the lobby doors just ahead of the theatergoers. They crossed the lobby, went out to the sidewalk, and the Ford was half a block away to their left, coming along behind a slow-cruising cab.

"God damn it," Van said. "What's the matter with Phil's timing?"

"He probably got stuck at a red light," Herman said.

The Ford slipped by the cab and stopped at their feet. They slid in, the sidewalk behind them filled with smokers, and Phil drove them casually but firmly away from there.

The two shopping bags were in the back with Herman and Jack—Van was up front now—and every time they went over a pothole the damn phone tinkled, which began to drive Herman up the wall. He was a compulsive phone answerer, and there was no way to answer this phone.

Also, the money was getting to him. He was glad to give his expertise to the Movement, help the Movement cover its expenses in the time-honored fashion of the IRA, but at times he could feel his palm itching to hold onto some of the cash he got for them this way. As he'd told his guests a little earlier tonight, he had expensive tastes.

It wouldn't be so bad if he had some private scores going, but it had been almost a year since he'd been involved in a non-political robbery, and the money from that last caper was just about gone. He needed something soon, or he'd be eating that black bread without the caviar.

They were heading up Central Park West when Phil said, "Do I hear a phone? I keep thinking I hear a phone."

Van said, "Jack stole their phone."

Herman could see Phil frowning as he drove. "He stole their phone? Just to be mean?"

"I need an extension for my bedroom," Jack said. "Lemme see if I can get it to be quiet." He took it out of the bag and held it in his lap, and it didn't tinkle as much after that.

Jack having moved the phone had dislodged some of the crumpled paper, and Herman could see green down in there. A hundred dollars, he thought, for expenses. But there was no point in it; a hundred dollars wouldn't come near his expenses.

They let him off across the street from his building. They headed on uptown, and Herman sprinted across the street and inside. He went around to the service elevator, rode it up to his floor, and pushed the 1 button to send it back down again when he got off. He entered his kitchen and Mrs. Olaffson said, "Everything's all right."

"Good."

"They're getting drunk."

"Very good. You can serve any time."

"Yes, sir."

He walked through the apartment to the living room and noted the shifts that had taken place in his absence. Several of them, but primarily involving George and Linda Lachine. George and Susan were sitting together now, George with a rather fatuous smile on his face while Susan talked to him, and Linda was standing over on the opposite side of the room, trying to look as though she were admiring the W. C. Fields print.

Rastus and Diane were still together, Rastus now with his hand on Diane's leg. The tinkling telephone and the reminder of his money worries had put Herman in a bad mood and left him feeling unable to cope with the complexities that Rastus would have to offer. So it was heterosexual time; why not?

First he had to make some general comments to the general group, who greeted his return with comments about how long he'd been away. "You know those people," he said with a dismissing wave of the hand. "They can't do anything on their own, not a thing."

"Problems?" Foster asked. He had come with Diane but seemed uninterested in leaving with her.

"Nothing they can't handle by themselves," he said and gave everybody a brisk grin as he rounded the coffee table and headed for Linda.

But he didn't get there. Mrs. Olaffson appeared again, in a rerun, complete with the same dialogue: "Telephone, sir."

Herman looked at her, for just a second too bewildered to speak. He couldn't say, "My call from the Coast?" because that was all over now. He very nearly said, "We've done that bit," but stopped himself in time. Finally, out of desperation, he said, "Who is it?"

"He just said it was a friend, sir."

"Listen," Rastus drawled in that Southern-cracker voice he liked to use when irritated, "ain't we never gonna eat?"

"All right," Herman said. To Rastus, to Mrs. Olaffson, to everybody. "I'll make this one fast," he promised grimly, strode from the room, went down the hall, and bashed his nose painfully when he turned the knob on the study door

without stopping and the door turned out still to be locked
"God *damn!*" he said, his eyes tearing and his nose smart-
ing. Holding his nose—he reminded himself of that usher—
he trotted around through the kitchen and into the study
that way. Dropping into the director's chair, he picked up
the receiver and said, "Yes!"

"Hello, Herman?"

"Yeah, that's right. Who's this?"

"Kelp."

Herman's spirits suddenly lifted. "Well, hello," he said
"Been a long time."

"You sound like you got a cold."

"No, I just hit my nose."

"What?"

"Never mind," Herman said. "What's happening?"

"Depends," Kelp said. "You available?"

"Never better."

"This is still a maybe."

"Which is better than a nothing," Herman said.

"That's true," Kelp said with some surprise, as though
he'd never thought that out before. "You know the O. J
Bar?"

"Sure."

"Tomorrow night, eight-thirty."

Herman frowned. There was a screening he'd been
invited to . . . No. As he'd told his guests, he had expensive
tastes, and as he'd told Kelp, a maybe was better than a
nothing. "I'll be there," he said.

"See you."

Herman hung up and reached for a Kleenex. Smiling
he wiped the tears from his eyes, then carefully unlocked
the study door and went out to the hall, where Mrs
Olaffson greeted him with "Dinner is ready, sir."

"And so am I," he said.

10

VICTOR stood smiling in the elevator. This building, on Park Avenue in the seventies, had been built at the turn of the century, but the elevator dated from 1926 and looked it. Victor had seen identical elevators in old movies—the dark wood, the waist-high brass rail, the smoke-tinted mirror, the corner light fixtures like brass skyscrapers upside down. Victor felt embraced by the era of the pulps and gazed around with a happy smile as he and his uncle rode up to the seventeenth floor.

Kelp said, "What the hell you grinning at?"

"I'm sorry," Victor said contritely. "I just liked the looks of the elevator."

"This is a medical doctor we're going to," Kelp said. "Not a psychiatrist."

"All right," Victor said soberly.

"And remember to let me do the talking."

Earnestly, Victor said, "Oh, I will."

He was finding this whole operation fascinating. Dortmunder had been perfect, Murch and his Mom had been perfect, the back room of the O. J. Bar and Grill had been perfect, and the steps being taken to put the job together were perfect. Even Dortmunder's obvious reluctance to let Victor participate was perfect; it was only right that the old pro wouldn't want to work with the rank amateur. But Victor knew that by the finish he would have had opportunity to demonstrate his value. The thought made him smile again, until he felt Kelp's eyes on him, when he immediately wiped the smile away.

"It's unusual that I'd even bring you along," Kelp said as the elevator door opened and they stepped out together into the seventeenth-floor foyer. The doctor's door, with a discreet name plate, was to the left. Kelp said, "He might not even want to talk in front of you."

"Oh, I hope not," Victor said, laughing boyishly.

"If he does," Kelp said, "you go right back to the waiting room. Don't argue with him."

"Oh, I wouldn't," Victor said sincerely.

Kelp grunted and went in, Victor following.

The nurse was behind a partition on the right. Victor stayed in the background while Kelp talked to her, saying, "We have an appointment. Charles Willis and Walter McLain."

"Yes, sir. If you'll just take a seat . . ." She pushed a buzzer that let them through the interior door.

The waiting room looked like the scale model of a Holiday Inn lobby. A stout lady looked up from her copy of *Weight Watchers* and gave them the glance of anonymous hostility with which people always look at one another in doctors' waiting rooms. Kelp and Victor pawed through the magazines on the central table, and Kelp sat down with a fairly recent *Newsweek*. Victor searched and searched, found nothing at all interesting, and finally settled for a copy of *Gourmet*. He sat down with it near Kelp, browsed along, and after a while noticed that the word "redolent" appeared on every page. He staved off boredom by watching for its reappearances.

But mostly he thought about the robbery and what he and Kelp were doing here. It had never occurred to him that big-scale robbers had to be financed, just like anybody else, but of course they did. The preparation of a robbery involved all sorts of expenses, and somebody had to foot the bill. Victor had eagerly asked Kelp a thousand questions about that facet of the operation and had learned that sometimes a member of the robbery team did the financing, in return for a larger share of the profit, but that more often the financing was done by outsiders, who put up the money for a guarantee of 100 percent profit, two dollars for every one, should the robbery turn out to be successful. If the robbery failed, of course, the financier got nothing.

"Mostly what we get," Kelp had said, "is undeclared

income. Doctors are the best, but florists are pretty good, too. Anybody whose line lets them keep some cash that they don't tell the Feds about. You'd be surprised how many greenbacks there are in safe-deposit boxes around the country. They're saving the money for when they retire. They can't really spend it now, for fear the income-tax people will get after them. They can't invest it any-place legal for the same reason. So it just sits there, not earning any interest, getting eaten up by inflation, and they look around for some way to put it to work. They'll go for a high risk if they can get a shot at a high return. And if they can be a silent partner."

"That's fascinating," Victor had said raptly.

"I like doctors best," Kelp had said. "I don't know why, I've just got a thing about doctors. I use their cars, I use their money. They've never let me down yet. You can trust doctors."

They spent half an hour now in this particular doctor's waiting room. The stout lady was called in by the nurse after a while and never returned. Nor did any other patient come out. Victor wondered about that, but later on discovered the doctor had a different exit, another door that led back to the elevator.

Finally the nurse came back, saying, "Doctor will see you now." Kelp followed the nurse, and Victor followed Kelp, and they all went down a hall to an examining room—white cabinets, black leatherette examination table. "Doctor will be right with you," the nurse said, and shut the door behind her when she left.

Kelp sat down on the examination table and let his feet dangle. "Now, let me do the talking."

"Oh, sure," Victor said reassuringly. He wandered around the room, reading the charts and the labels on the bottles, until the door opened again and the doctor came in.

"Doctor Osbertson," said Kelp, getting to his feet. "This is my nephew, Victor. He's okay."

Victor smiled at Dr. Osbertson. The doctor was fiftyish, distinguished-looking, well padded and irritable. He had the round face of a sulky baby, and he said, "I'm not sure I want to be involved in this sort of thing any more."

Kelp said, "Well, that's up to you. It looks like a good one, though."

"The way the market's been . . ." He looked around, as though he'd never seen his own examining room before and didn't much like it. "There's no place to sit in here," he said. "Come with me."

They followed him part way back along the same hall and into a small wood-paneled office with two maroon chairs facing the desk. All three sat down, and the doctor leaned back in his swivel chair, frowning in discontent. "I took a couple of headers in the market," he said. "Take my advice. Never listen to a stock tip from a terminal case. What if he turns out to be wrong?"

"Yeah, I guess so," Kelp said.

"Then my car was stolen."

Victor looked at Kelp, who was facing the doctor, his expression showing sympathetic interest. "Is that right?"

"Just the other day. Kids, joy-riding. Managed to get into a rear-end collision somehow."

"Kids, huh? Did they get them?"

"The police?" The doctor's sullen baby face made a grimacing smile, as though he had gas. "Don't make me laugh. They never get anybody."

"Let's hope not," Kelp said. "But about our proposition."

"Then I had to buy some letters back." The doctor waggled his hands, as though to minimize what he was saying. "Ex-patient," he said. "Didn't mean a thing, of course, just consolation in her grief."

"The terminal tipper's wife?"

"What? No, I never wrote *her* anything, thank God. This one . . . Well, it doesn't matter. Expenses have been high. That car business was the last straw."

"Did you leave the keys in it?"

"Of course not." He sat up straight to show how indignant he was.

"But you're insured," Kelp said.

"You never recover all your costs," the doctor said.

"Traveling by cab, making phone calls, getting estimates . . . I'm a busy man. I don't have time for all this. And now you people. What if you're caught?"

"We'll do our best to avoid that."

"But what if you are? Then I'm out—how much do you want?"

"We figure four thousand."

The doctor pursed his lips. He looked now like a baby who'd just had his pacifier plucked from him. "A lot of money," he said.

"Eight thousand back."

"If it works."

"This is a good one," Kelp said. "You know I can't tell you the details, but—"

The doctor flung up his hands as though to ward off an avalanche. "Don't tell me. I don't want to know! I won't be an accessory!"

"Sure," Kelp said. "I know how you feel. Anyway, we think of this one as being a really sure thing. Money in the bank, you might say."

The doctor rested his palms on his green blotter. "Four thousand, you say."

"There might be a little more. I don't think so."

"You're getting the whole thing from me?"

"If we can."

"This recession . . ." He shook his head. "People don't come around for every little thing any more. When I see a patient in the waiting room these days, I know that patient is *sick*. Drug companies getting a little stingier, too. Had to dip into capital just the other week."

"That's a shame," Kelp said.

"Diet foods," the doctor said. "There's another problem. Used to be, I could count on gastritis from overeating for a good thirty percent of my income. Now everybody's on diets. How do they expect a doctor to make ends meet?"

"Things sure can get rough," Kelp said.

"And now they're giving up cigarettes. The lungs have been a gold mine for me for years. But not any more." He shook his head. "I don't know what medicine is coming to," he said. "If I had a son entering college today, and he asked me if I wanted him to follow in my footsteps, I'd say, 'No, son. I want you to be a tax accountant. That's the wave of the future, you ride it. It's too late for me.' That's what I'd tell him."

"Good advice," Kelp said.

The doctor slowly shook his head. "Four thousand," he said.

"That should do it, yes."

"All right." He sighed and got to his feet. "Wait here. I'll get it for you."

He left the room, and Kelp turned to Victor to say, "He left the keys in it."

11

DORTMUNDER at the movies was like a rock on the beach; the story kept washing over him, in wave after wave, but never had any effect. This one, called *Murphy's Madrigal,* had been advertised as a tragic farce and gave the audience an opportunity to try out every emotion known to the human brain. Pratfalls, crippled children, Nazis, doomed lovers, you never knew what was going to happen next.

And Dortmunder just sat there. Beside him May roared with laughter, she sobbed, she growled with rage, she clutched his arm and cried, "Oh!" And Dortmunder just sat there.

When they got out of the movie it was ten to eight, so they had time to get a hero. They went to a Blimpie and May treated, and when they were sitting together at a table with their sandwiches under the bright lights she said, "You didn't like it."

"Sure I did," he said. He pushed bread and sauerkraut in his mouth with his finger.

"You just sat there."

"I liked it," he said. Going to the movies had been her idea; he'd spent most of the time in the theater thinking about that mobile home bank out on Long Island and how to take it away.

"Tell me what you liked about it."

He thought hard, trying to remember something he'd seen. "The color," he said.

"A part of the *movie*."

She was really getting irritated now, which he didn't want to happen. He struggled and came up with a memory. "The elevator bit," he said. The director of the movie had tied a strong elastic around a camera and dropped the camera down a brightly lighted elevator shaft. The thing had recoiled just before hitting bottom and had bounced up and down for quite a while before coming to rest. The whole sequence, forty-three seconds of it, was run without a break in the movie, and audiences had been known to throw up en masse at that point in the picture. Everybody agreed it was great, the high point of film art up to this time.

May smiled. "Okay," she said. "That *was* good, wasn't it?"

"Sure," he said. He looked at his watch.

"You got time. Eight-thirty, right?"

"Right."

"How does it look?"

He shrugged. "Possible. Crazy, but possible." Then, to keep her from going back to the subject of the movie and asking him more questions about it, he said, "There's still a lot of things to work out. But we maybe got a lockman."

"That's good."

"We still don't have anyplace to take it."

"You'll find a place."

"It's pretty big," he said.

"So's the world."

He looked at her, not sure she'd just said something

sensible, but decided to let it go. "There's also financing," he said.

"Is that going to be a problem?"

"I don't think so. Kelp saw somebody today." He hadn't known May very long, so this was the first time she'd watched him put together a piece of work, but he had a feeling with her as though she just naturally understood the situation. He never gave her a lot of background explanations, and she didn't seem to need any. It was very relaxing. In a funny way, May reminded Dortmunder of his ex-wife, not because she was similar but because she was so very different. It was the contrast that did it. Until he'd started up with May, Dortmunder hadn't even thought about his former wife for years. A show-biz performer she'd been, with the professional name of Honeybun Bazoom. Dortmunder had married her in San Diego in 1952 on his way to Korea—the only police action he'd ever been in on the side of the police—and had divorced her in Reno in 1954 on his way out of the Army. Honeybun had mostly been interested in Honeybun, but if something outside herself *did* attract her attention she was immediately full of questions about it. She could ask more questions than a kid at the zoo. Dortmunder had answered the first few thousand, until he'd realized that none of the answers ever stayed inside that round head.

May couldn't have been more different; she never asked the questions, and she always held onto the answers.

Now, they finished their heroes and left the Blimpie, and on the sidewalk May said, "I'll take the subway."

"Take a cab."

She had a fresh cigarette in the corner of her mouth, having lit it after finishing eating. "Naw," she said. "I'll take the subway. A cab after a hero gives me heartburn."

"You want to come along to the O. J?"

"Naw, you go ahead."

"The other night, Murch brought his Mom."

"I'd rather go home."

Dortmunder shrugged. "Okay. I'll see you later."

"See you later."

She slopped away down the street, and Dortmunder headed the other way. He still had time, so he decided to walk, which meant going through Central Park. He walked along the cinder path alone, and under a street light a shifty-eyed stocky guy in a black turtle-neck sweater came out of nowhere and said, "Excuse me."

Dortmunder stopped. "Yeah?"

"I'm taking a survey," the guy said. His eyes danced a little, and he seemed to be grinning and yet not to be grinning. It was the same kind of expression most of the people in the movie had had. He said, "Here you are, you're a citizen, you're walking along in the park at night. What would you do if somebody came along and mugged you?"

Dortmunder looked at him. "I'd beat his head in," he said.

The guy blinked, and the almost grin disappeared. He looked slightly confused, and he said, "What if he had, uh, well, what if he was . . ." Then he shook his head, waggled both hands and backed off, saying, "Nah, forget it. Doesn't matter, forget it."

"Okay," Dortmunder said. He walked on through the park and over to Amsterdam and up to the O. J. When he went in, Rollo was having a discussion with the only two customers, a pair of overweight commission salesmen in the auto-parts line, about whether sexual intercourse after a heavy meal was medically good or medically bad. They were supporting their arguments mostly with personal anecdotes, and Rollo obviously had trouble breaking himself free from the conversation. Dortmunder waited at the end of the bar, and finally Rollo said, "Now, hold it now, hold it a second. Don't start that yet. I'll be right back." Then he came down the bar, handed Dortmunder the bottle called Amsterdam Liquor Store Bourbon—"Our Own Brand" plus two glasses, and said, "All that's here so far is the draft beer and salt. His mother let him out by himself tonight."

"There'll be more coming," Dortmunder said. "I don't know how many."

"The more the merrier," Rollo said sourly and went back to his discussion.

In the back room, Murch was sprinkling salt in his beer to restore the head. He looked up at Dortmunder's entrance and said, "How you doing?"

"Fine," Dortmunder said. He put the bottle and glasses on the table and sat down.

"I made better time tonight," Murch said. "I tried a different route."

"Is that right?" Dortmunder opened the bottle.

"I went down Flatlands and up *Remsen,*" Murch said. "Not Rockaway Parkway, see? Then I went over Empire Boulevard and up Bedford Avenue all the way into Queens and took the Williamsburg Bridge over into Manhattan."

Dortmunder poured. "Is that right?" he said. He was just waiting for Murch to stop talking, because he had something to say to him.

"Then Delancey and Allen and right up First Avenue and across town at Seventy-ninth Street. Worked like a dream."

"Is that right?" Dortmunder said. He sipped at his drink and said, "You know, Rollo's kind of unhappy about you."

Murch looked surprised, but eager to please. "Why? Cause I parked out front?"

"No. A customer that comes in and nurses one beer all night long, it doesn't do too much for his business."

Murch glanced down at his beer, and then looked very pained. "I never thought of that," he said.

"I just figured I'd mention it."

"The thing is, I don't like to drink and drive. That's why I space it out."

Dortmunder had nothing to say to that.

Murch pondered and finally said hopefully, "What if I bought *him* a drink? Would that do it?"

"Could be."

"Let me give it a try," Murch said, and as he got to his feet the door opened and Kelp and Victor came in. The room was very small and very full of table anyway, so it

took a while to bring Kelp and Victor in while getting
Murch out, and during that time Dortmunder brooded at
Victor. It seemed to him that Victor was becoming more
and more an accepted part of this job, which he didn't
much like but couldn't quite find the way to stop. Kelp
was doing it, but he was doing it in such a sneaky quiet
fashion that Dortmunder never had a clear moment when
he could say, "Okay, cut it out." But how could anybody
expect him to go steal a bank with some clown *smiling* at
him all the time?

Murch finally shot himself out of the room, like a dollop
of toothpaste squeezed out of a tube, and Kelp said, "I see
Herman isn't here yet."

"You talked to him?"

"He's interested."

Dortmunder brooded some more. Kelp himself was all
right, but he tended to surround himself with people and
operations that were just a little off. Victor, for instance.
And now bringing in some guy named Herman X. What
could you hope for from somebody named Herman X?
Had he ever *done* anything in this line? If he was going to
turn out to be another smiler, Dortmunder was just going
to have to put his foot down. Enough smiling is enough.

Sitting down next to Dortmunder and reaching for the
bourbon bottle, Kelp said, "We got the financing set."

Victor had taken the spot directly across from Dortmun-
der. He was smiling. Shading his eyes with his hand,
Dortmunder ducked his head a little and said to Kelp,
"You got the full four grand?"

"Every penny. The light too bright for you?"

"I just went to a movie."

"Oh, yeah? What'd you see?"

Dortmunder had forgotten the title. "It was in color," he
said.

"That narrows it. Probably a pretty recent one, then."

"Yeah."

Victor said, "I'm drinking tonight." He sounded very
pleased.

Dortmunder ducked his head a little more and looked
at Victor under his fingers. He was smiling, of course, and

holding up a tall glass. It was pink. Dortmunder said, "Oh, yeah?"

"A sloe-gin fizz," Victor said.

"Is that right?" Dortmunder readjusted head and fingers —it was like putting down venetian blinds—and turned firmly back to Kelp. "So you got the whole four thousand," he said.

"Yeah. A funny thing about that . . ."

The door opened and Murch came back in. "It's all set," he said. He was smiling, too, but it was easier to live with than Victor's. "Thanks for setting me straight," he said.

"Glad it worked out," Dortmunder said.

Murch sat down in front of his beer and carefully salted it. "Rollo's okay when you get to know him," he said.

"Sure he is."

"Drives a Saab."

Dortmunder had known Rollo for years but hadn't known about the Saab. "Is that right?" he said.

"Used to drive a Borg-Ward. Sold it because he couldn't get parts when they stopped making the car."

Kelp said, "What kind of car is that?"

"Borg-Ward. German. Same company that makes Norge refrigerators."

"They're American."

"The refrigerators, yeah. The cars were German."

Dortmunder finished his drink and reached for the bottle, and Rollo opened the door and stuck his head in to say, "There's an Old Crow on the rocks out here asking for Kelp."

"That's him now," Kelp said.

"A darkish fella."

"That's him," Kelp said. "Send him on in."

"Right." Rollo gave a bartender's glance around the table. "Everybody set?"

They all murmured.

Rollo cocked an eye at Murch. "Stan, you got enough salt?"

"Oh, sure," Murch said. "Thanks a lot, Rollo."

"Any time, Stan."

Rollo went away. Dortmunder glanced at Murch, but

didn't say anything, and a minute later a tall lean guy with a dark-brown complexion and a very modest Afro came into the room. What he looked most like was an Army second lieutenant on leave. He was nodding slightly and grinning slightly as he came in and shut the door, and Dortmunder wondered at first if he was on something; then he realized it was just the self-protective cool of somebody meeting a group of people for the first time.

"Hey, Herman," Kelp said.

"Hey," agreed Herman quietly. He closed the door behind him and stood there jiggling ice in his old-fashioned glass, like an early arrival at a cocktail party.

Kelp made the introductions: "Herman X, this is Dortmunder, that's Stan Murch, that's my nephew Victor."

"How are ya."

"Hello, Mr. X."

Dortmunder watched Herman frown slightly at Victor and then glance at Kelp. Kelp, however, was busy being host, saying, "Take a seat, Herman. We were just talking about the situation."

"That's what I want to hear about," Herman said. He sat down to Dortmunder's right. "The situation."

Dortmunder said, "I'm surprised I don't know you."

Herman gave him a grin. "We probably travel in different circles."

"I was just wondering what your experience is."

Herman's grin broadened into a smile. "Well, now," he said. "One doesn't like to talk about one's experiences in front of a whole room of witnesses."

Kelp said, "Everybody's okay in here. But, Dortmunder, Herman really does know his business."

Dortmunder continued to frown at Herman. It seemed to him there was something of the dilettante about this guy. Your ordinary run-of-the-mill heavy could be a dilettante, but a lockman was supposed to be serious, he was supposed to be a man with a craft, with expertise.

Herman glanced around the table with an ironic smile, then shrugged, sipped at his drink and said, "Well, last night I helped take away the *Justice* receipts."

Victor, looking startled, said, "From the Bureau?"

Herman looked baffled. "From the bureau? It was on tables; they were counting it."

Kelp said, "That was you? I read about that in the paper."

So had Dortmunder. He said, "What locks did you open?"

"None," Herman said. "It wasn't that kind of a job."

Victor, still trying to work it all out, said, "You mean down at Foley Square?"

This time, Herman's frown was deep and somewhat hostile. "Well, the FBI is down there," he said.

"The Bureau," said Victor.

Kelp said, "Later, Victor. You're confused."

"They don't *have* any receipts at the Bureau," Victor said. "I should know. I was an agent for twenty-one months."

Herman was on his feet, the chair tipping over behind him. "What's going on here?"

"It's all right," Kelp said, fast and soothing. He patted the air in a gesture of reassurance. "It's all right. They fired him."

Herman, in his mistrust, was trying to look in seven directions at once; his eyes kept almost crossing. "If this is entrapment—" he said.

"They fired him," Kelp insisted. "Didn't they, Victor?"

"Well," Victor said, "we sort of agreed to disagree. I wasn't exactly fired precisely, not exactly."

Herman had focused on Victor again, and now he said, "You mean it was political?"

Before Victor could answer, Kelp said smoothly, "Something like that. Yeah, it was political, *wasn't it, Victor?*"

"Uh. Sure, yeah. You could call it . . . I guess you could call it that."

Herman shrugged his shoulders inside his sports jacket, to adjust it. Then he sat down again with a relieved smile, saying, "You had me going there for a minute."

Dortmunder had learned patience at great cost. The trial and error of life among human beings had taught him that whenever a bunch of them began to jump up and down and shout at cross-purposes, the only thing a sane man could do was sit back and let them sort it out for themselves. No matter how long it took. The alternative was to try to attract their attention, either with explanations of the misunderstanding or with a return to the original topic of conversation, and to make that attempt meant that sooner or later you too would be jumping up and down and shouting at cross-purposes. Patience, patience; at the very worst, they would finally wear themselves out.

Now, he looked around the table at everybody smiling in new comprehension—Murch was salting his beer again —and then he said, "What we had in mind for this job was a lockman."

"That's what I am," Herman said. "Last night, I was just filling in. You know, helping out. Usually I'm a lockman."

"For instance."

"For instance the People's Co-operative Supermarket on Sutter Avenue about three weeks ago. The Lenox Avenue office of the Tender Loving Care Loan Company a couple weeks before that. Smilin Sam Tahachapee's safe in the horse room behind the Fifth of November Bar and Grill on Linden Boulevard two days before that. The Balmy Breeze Hotel safe in Atlantic City during the Retired Congressmen's Convention the week before that. The Open Hand Check Cashing Agency on Jerome Avenue the—"

"You don't *need* work," Kelp said. He sounded awed. "You got all the work you can handle."

"Not to mention money," Murch said.

Herman shook his head with a bitter smile. "The fact is," he said, "I'm broke. I really need a score."

Dortmunder said, "You must run through it pretty quick."

"Those are Movement jobs," Herman said. "I don't get to keep any of it."

This time Victor was the only one who understood. "Ah," he said. "You're helping to finance their schemes."

"Like the free-lunch program," Herman said.

Kelp said, "Wait a minute. These are Movement jobs, so you don't get to keep the money. What does that *mean* exactly? Movement jobs. You mean they're like for practice? You send the money back?"

Victor said, "He gives the money to the organization he belongs to." Mildly, he said to Herman, "Which movement do you belong to, exactly?"

"One of them," Herman said. To Kelp he said, "I don't set any of those things up. These people that I believe in"—with a glance at Victor—"that your nephew would know about, they set them up, and they put together the group that does the job. What we say is, we're *liberating* the money."

"I think of it the other way around," Kelp said. "I think of it that I'm capturing the money."

Dortmunder said, "What was the last job you did on your own? Where you got to keep the loot?"

"About a year ago," Herman said. "A bank in St. Louis."

"Who'd you work with?"

"Stan Devers and Mort Kobler. George Cathcart drove."

"I know George," Kelp said.

Dortmunder knew Kobler. "All right," he said.

"Now," Herman said, "let's talk about you boys. Not what you've done, I'll take Kelp's word for that. What you want to do."

Dortmunder took a deep breath. He wasn't happy about this moment. "We're going to steal a bank," he said.

Herman looked puzzled. "Rob a bank?"

"Steal a bank." To Kelp he said, "You tell him."

Kelp told him. At first Herman sort of grinned, as though waiting for the punch line. Then, for a while, he frowned, as though suspecting he was surrounded by mental cases. And finally he looked interested, as though the idea had caught his fancy. At the end he said, "So I can take my time. I can even work in daylight if I want."

"Sure," Kelp said.

Herman nodded. He looked at Dortmunder and said, "Why is it still just a maybe?"

"We don't have any place to put it," Dortmunder said. "Also, we have to get wheels for it."

"I'm working on that," Murch said. "But I may need some help."

"A whole bank," Herman said. He beamed. "We're gonna liberate a whole bank."

Kelp said, "We're gonna *capture* a whole bank."

"It comes to the same thing," Herman told him. "Believe me, it comes to the same thing."

12

MURCH'S Mom stood smiling and blinking in the sunlight in front of Kresge's holding her purse strap with both hands, arms extended down and in front of her so that the purse dangled at her knees. She was wearing a dress with horizontal green and yellow stripes which did nothing to improve her figure, and below that yellow vinyl boots with green laces all the way up. Above the dress she wore her neck brace. The purse was an ordinary beige leather affair, which went much better with the neck brace than with the dress and boots.

Standing next to a parking meter, peering at Murch's Mom's image in an Instamatic camera, was May, dressed in her usual fashion. The original idea was that May would be the one in the fancy clothes and Murch's Mom would take the pictures, but May had absolutely refused to buy the kind of dress and boots Dortmunder had in mind. It also turned out that Murch's Mom was one of those people who always take pictures low and to the left of what they were aiming at. So the roles had been reversed.

May kept frowning into the camera, apparently never being quite content with what she saw—which was perfectly understandable. Shoppers would come along the sidewalk, see Murch's Mom posing there, see May with the camera, and would pause a second, not wanting to louse up the picture. But then nothing would happen except that May would frown some more and maybe take a step to the left or right, so the shoppers would all finally murmur, "Excuse me," or something like that and duck on by.

At last May looked up from the camera and shook her head, saying, "The light's no good here. Let's try farther down the block."

"Okay," said Murch's Mom. She and May started down the sidewalk together, and Murch's Mom said under her breath, "I feel like a damn fool in this get-up."

"You look real nice," May said.

"I know what I look like," Murch's Mom said grimly. "I look like the Good Humor flavor of the month. Lemon pistachio."

"Let's try here," May said. Coincidentally, they were in front of the bank.

"Okay," Murch's Mom said.

"You stand against the wall in the sunlight," May said.

"Okay."

Murch's Mom backed up slowly across the brick rubble toward the trailer, and May backed up against the car parked there. This time, Murch's Mom held the purse at her side, and her back was against the trailer wall. May took a fast picture, then stepped forward two paces and took a second one. With the third, she was at the inner edge of the sidewalk—too close to get all of Murch's Mom in the picture and with the camera angled too low to include her head.

"There," May said. "I think that's got it."

"Thank you, dear," Murch's Mom said, smiling, and the two ladies walked around the block.

13

DORTMUNDER and Kelp quartered around the remoter bits of Long Island like a bird dog who's lost his bird. Today's car was an orange Datsun 240Z with the usual MD plates. They drove around under a sky that kept threatening rain but never quite delivered, and after a while Dortmunder began to grouse. "In the meantime," he said, "I'm not making any income."

"You've got May."

"I don't like living on the earnings of a woman," Dortmunder said. "It isn't in my makeup."

"The earnings of a woman? She's not a hooker, she's a cashier."

"The principle's the same."

"The interest isn't. What's that over there?"

"Looks like a barn," Dortmunder said, squinting.

"Abandoned?"

"How the hell do I know?"

"Let's take a look."

They looked that day at seven barns, none of them abandoned. They also looked at a quonset hut that had most recently contained a computer-parts factory which had gone broke, but the interior was a jumble of desks and machinery and parts and junk, too crowded and filthy to be useful. They also looked at an airplane hangar in front of a pock-marked blacktop landing strip—a onetime flying school, now abandoned, but occupied by a hippie commune, as Dortmunder and Kelp discovered when they parked out front. The hippies had mistaken them for representatives of the sheriff's office and right away began shouting about squatters' rights and demonstrations and all and didn't stop shouting until after Dortmunder and Kelp got back in the car and drove away again.

This was the third day of the search. Days one and two had been similar.

Victor's car was a black 1938 Packard limousine, with the bulky trunk and the divided rear window and the long coffin-like hood and the headlights sitting up on top of the arrogant broad fenders. The upholstery was scratchy gray plush, and there were leather thongs to hold onto next to the doors on the inside and small green vases containing artificial flowers hanging in little wire racks between the doors.

Victor drove, and Herman sat beside him and stared out at the countryside. "This is ridiculous," he said. "There's got to be *something* you can hide a trailer in."

Casually, Victor said, "What newspapers do you read mostly, Herman?"

Dortmunder walked into the apartment and sat down on the sofa and stared moodily at the turned-off television set. May, the cigarette in the corner of her mouth, slopped in from the kitchen. "Anything?"

"With the encyclopedias," Dortmunder said, staring at the TV, "I could've picked up maybe seventy bucks out there today. Maybe a hundred."

"I'll get you a beer," May said. She went back to the kitchen.

Murch's Mom brooded over the pictures. "I never looked so foolish in my life," she said.

"That isn't the point, Mom."

She tapped the one in which she appeared headless. "At least there you can't tell it's me."

Her son was hunched over the three color photographs on the dining-room table, counting. The lace holes in the boots and the stripes on the dress made a ruler. Murch counted, added, compared, got totals for each of the three pictures, and at last said, "Thirty-seven and a half inches high."

"You sure?"

"Positive. Thirty-seven and a half inches high."

"Can I burn those pictures now?"

"Sure," Murch said. She gathered up the pictures, and as she hurried from the room he called, "Did you get rid of that dress?"

"You know it!" she sang out. She sounded almost gay.

"The way I figure it," Herman said, riding along in Victor's car, scanning the countryside for large abandoned buildings, "what we got to deal with here is three hundred years of slavery."

"Myself," Victor said, pushing the Packard slowly toward Montauk Point, "I've never really been political."

"You were in the FBI."

"That wasn't for politics. I always thought of myself as being involved in adventure. You know what I mean?"

Herman gave him a quizzical look and then a slow grin. "Yeah," he said. "Yeah, I know what you mean."

"For me, adventure meant the FBI."

"Yeah, that's right! See, for me, it was the Movement."

"Sure," Victor said.

"Naturally," said Herman.

"I don't like that sound," Murch said. Sitting there behind the wheel, head cocked, listening to the engine, he looked like a squirrel driving a car.

"You're supposed to be looking for abandoned buildings," his Mom said. She herself was turning her head slowly back and forth, like a Navy pilot looking for shipwreck survivors.

"You hear it? Ting, ting, ting. You hear it?"

"What's that over there?"

"What?"

"I said, what's that over there?"

"Looks like some kind of church."

"Let's go look at it."

Murch turned in that direction. "Keep your eye peeled for a gas station," he said.

This current car—he'd had it seven months—had started life as an American Motors Javelin, but since he'd owned it Murch had changed some things. By now, looks aside, it bore about as much similarity to a Javelin as to a javelin. It growled like some very large and savage but sleepy beast as Murch steered it through bumpy streets of prewar one-family housing toward the church with the sagging roof.

They stopped out front. The lawn was weedy, the wooden walls needed painting very badly, and a few of the window panes were broken. "Let's take a look," Murch's Mom said.

Murch shut off the ignition and listened attentively to the silence for a few seconds, as though that too could tell him something. Then he said, "Okay," and he and his Mom got out of the car.

Inside, the church was very dim; nevertheless, the priest sweeping the central aisle saw them at once and hurried toward them, clutching his broom at port arms. "Yes? Yes? Can I help you?"

Murch said, "Never mind," and turned away.

His Mom explained, "We were wondering if this place was abandoned."

The priest nodded. "Almost," he said, looking around. "Almost."

"I think I have an idea," May said.

Kelp said, "Excuse me, Miss. I wanted to open an account."

The girl, her head bent beneath a towering bouffant hairdo, didn't pause in her typing. "Have a seat, and an officer will be right with you."

"Thank you," Kelp said. He sat down and glanced around the interior of the bank, as a bored man will do while waiting.

The safe was down at the Kresge end and more impressive-looking than Victor had implied. It filled practically the whole width of the trailer down there at the end, and the door—which was ajar—was admirably large and thick.

The customer portion of the bank was separated from the rest by a chest-high partition, with here and there an entrance door through it. If one were to take the top off the trailer and look inside, this chest-high partition would form a letter C, long and thin and with right angles instead of curves. The customer area was the part enclosed by the C—the right half of the middle of the trailer. At the top of the C was the safe, down along the side of the C were the tellers, and the thick bottom of the C contained the desks of the three bank officers. The girl in the bouffant hairdo was at a smaller desk outside the C; she and the elderly bank guard were the only employees in the customer section.

Kelp cased the joint, and then he memorized it, and then he got up and read the pamphlets for auto loans and credit cards, and then he looked around the place again to be sure he remembered it all, and he remembered it all. He'd planned on actually opening an account, but finally that seemed superfluous, so he got to his feet and told the girl, "I'll come back after lunch."

The hairdo nodded. She kept typing.

"Why," Herman said, "from the outside it looks like any other garage."

Victor nodded, smiling. "I thought you'd like it," he said.

Dortmunder came out of the bedroom wearing black sneakers, black trousers and a long-sleeved black shirt. In one hand he was holding a black cap, and over his forearm hung a black leather jacket. May, who was hemming curtains, looked up and said, "You off?"

"Be back pretty soon."

"Break a leg," May said and went back to her sewing.

14

THE railroad-station parking lot had cars in it all night long on weekends, and this was Friday night, so there was no problem. Victor and Herman arrived in Victor's Packard, parked it and strolled over to the waiting room. This was the Long Island Railroad, which had been the best in the world since November of 1969. The waiting room was open and lit, since late trains came out here from the city on Friday nights, but the ticket office was closed. Victor and Herman wandered around the empty waiting room reading the notices until they saw headlights; then they went back outside.

It was the Javelin, growling contentedly to itself as though it had just eaten a Pinto. Murch was driving and Dortmunder was beside him. Murch slipped the Javelin into a parking space—it was done like a samurai sheathing his sword, the same sense of ceremony—and then he and Dortmunder got out and walked over to join the other two.

Dortmunder said, "Kelp isn't here yet?"

Victor said, "Do you suppose he had some trouble?"

"Here he comes," Herman said.

"I wonder what he brought me," Murch said as the truck headlights made the turn into the parking lot.

The town all around them was fairly well lit but basically empty, like a movie set. Traffic was light to moderate with people homeward bound from their Friday-night outings, and the occasional Nassau County police car was interested in drunken drivers, automobile accidents and potential burglary of downtown stores, not vehicles moving in and out of the railroad-station parking lot.

Kelp pulled to a stop next to the waiting men. His style of driving was in deep contrast with Murch, who seemed to do no physical labor at all but to operate his cars by thought control. Kelp, on the other hand, even after the truck had come to a stop, could still be seen in there for several seconds turning the wheel and shifting the gears, pushing and pulling and shoving and only gradually himself coming to a stop, like a radio that keeps broadcasting for a few seconds after you switch it off, while the tubes cool.

"Well," said Murch, in the manner of a man withholding judgment but not expecting much.

It was a good-sized truck, a Dodge, with a box about fifteen feet long. The doors and sides carried the company name: *Laurentian Paper Mills*. In addition, the doors bore the names of two cities: "Toronto, Ontario—Syracuse, New York." The cab was green, the box dark brown, and it had New York plates. Kelp had left the motor running, and it *gug-gugged* like any truck engine.

Now, as Kelp opened the door and climbed down to the pavement, carrying a brown shopping bag, Murch said to him, "What was it attracted you to this thing? In particular, I mean."

"The fact that it was empty," Kelp said. "We don't have to unload any paper."

Murch nodded. "Well," he said, "it'll do."

"There was an International Harvester I saw," Kelp told him, "with a nice racing stripe on it, but it was full of model cars."

"This one'll do," Murch said.

"If you want, I'll go back and get that one."

"No," Murch said judiciously, "this one will do just fine."

Kelp looked at Dortmunder and said, "I don't believe I've ever met such an ingrate in my life."

"Let's go," Dortmunder said.

Dortmunder and Kelp and Victor and Herman got up into the back of the truck, and Murch closed the van doors after them. Now the interior was pitch-black. Dortmunder felt his way to the side wall and sat down, as the others were already doing. A second later, the truck lurched forward.

The worst moment was the bump coming out of the parking lot. After that, Murch moved them along pretty smoothly.

In the dark, Dortmunder wrinkled his nose and sniffed. "Somebody's been drinking," he said.

Nobody answered.

"I can smell it," Dortmunder said. "Somebody had a drink."

"I can smell it, too," Kelp said. From the sound of his voice, he was just across the way.

Victor said, "Is that what that is? A funny smell, almost sweet."

Herman said, "Smells like whiskey. Not Scotch, though."

"Not bourbon either," Kelp said.

"The question is," Dortmunder said, "who's been drinking?" Because it was a very bad idea to drink while out on a job.

"Not me," Kelp said.

Herman said, "That's not my style."

There was a little silence, and suddenly Victor said, "Me? Heck, no!"

Dortmunder said, "Well, *somebody's* been drinking."

Herman said, "What do you want to do, smell everybody's breath?"

"I can smell it from here," Dortmunder said.

"The air is full of it," Kelp said.

All at once Herman said, "Wait a second. Wait a second, I think I know . . . Just wait a second." From the scrambling sound, he was getting to his feet, moving along the wall. Dortmunder waited, squinting his eyes in the darkness but still unable to see a thing.

A thudding. Herman: "Oops."

Victor: "Ow!"

Herman: "Sorry."

Victor (garbled a bit, as though he had fingers in his mouth): "That's okay."

Then there was a hollow drumming sound, and Herman

laughed. "Sure!" he said, obviously pleased with himself.
"You know what it is?"

"No," Dortmunder said. He was getting very irritated
that the drinker wouldn't own up to what he'd done and
starting to suspect it was Herman, now trying to distract
them all from the question with a lot of foolishness.

Herman said, "It's Canadian!"

Kelp sniffed loudly and said, "By God, I think you're
right. Canadian whiskey."

More hollow drumming, and Herman said, "This is a
fake wall. Up here behind the cab, it's a fake wall. We're
in a goddam smuggler's truck!"

Dortmunder said, "What?"

"That's where the smell's coming from, back there.
They must have broken a bottle."

Dortmunder said, "Smuggling? Prohibition's over."

"By golly, Herman," Victor said excitedly, "you've
stumbled on something important!" Never had he sounded
more like an FBI man.

Dortmunder said, "Prohibition's *over.*"

"Import duties," Victor explained. "That isn't directly
the Bureau's responsibility, that's Treasury's department,
but I do know a bit about it. There are outfits like this
strung all across the border. They smuggle Canadian
whiskey into the States and American cigarettes up into
Canada, and they make a pretty profit in both directions."

"Well, I'll be," said Kelp.

"Uncle," Victor said, "where exactly did you get this
truck?"

Kelp said, "You're not in the Bureau any more, Victor."

"Oh," Victor said. He sounded slightly confused. Then
he said, "Of course not. I was just wondering."

"In Greenpoint."

"Of course," Victor said musingly. "Down by the
piers."

There was another thud, and Herman cried, "Ouch! Son
of a *bitch!*"

Dortmunder called, "What happened?"

"Hurt my thumb. But I figured out how to get it open."

Kelp said, "Any whiskey in there?"

Dortmunder said warningly, "Wait a minute."

"For later," Kelp said.

A match flared. They could see Herman leaning through a narrow partition in the front wall, holding the match ahead of himself so they could make him out only in silhouette. "Cigarettes," Herman said. "About half full of cigarettes."

Kelp said, "True?"

"Swear to God."

"What *brand?*"

"L and M."

"No," Kelp said. "I'm not mature enough for them."

"Wait, there's some others. Uhhh, Salem."

"No. I feel like a dirty old man when I try to smoke a Salem. Springtime fresh and all, girls in covered bridges."

"Virginia Slims."

"What?"

"Sorry."

"That's May's brand," Dortmunder said. "I'll take some of them with me."

Kelp said, "I thought May got them free at the store."

"That's right, she does."

"Ow," Herman said, and the match went out. "Burned my finger."

"You better sit down," Dortmunder told him. "You're choppin' up your hands pretty good for somebody's gonna open some locks."

"Right," Herman said.

They rode along in silence awhile, and then Herman said, "You know, it really stinks in here."

Kelp said, "Everything happens to me. I looked at this truck, it said 'paper' on the side, I figured it would be nice and clean and neat."

"It really smells bad," Herman said.

"I wish Murch wouldn't jounce so much," Victor said. He sounded small and distant.

Dortmunder said, "How come?"

"I think I'm gonna be sick."

"Wait," Dortmunder urged him. "It's only a little far-ther."

"It's the smell," Victor said miserably. "And the jounc-ing."

"I'm beginning to feel that way, too," Kelp said. He didn't sound healthy.

Now that the idea had been suggested, Dortmunder too was starting to feel queasy. "Herman," he said, "maybe you ought to rap on the front wall, signal Murch to stop a minute."

"I don't think I can get up," Herman said. He too was sounding very unhappy.

Dortmunder swallowed. Then he swallowed again "Just a little longer," he said in a strangled voice and kept on swallowing.

Up front, Murch drove along in blissful ignorance. He was the one who'd found this place, and he'd worked out the fastest and smoothest route to reach it. Now he saw it, up ahead, the tall green fence around the yard, sur-mounted by the sign reading, "Lafferty's Mobile Homes—New, Used, Rebuilt, Repaired." He slowed to a stop in the darkness just beyond the main entrance, got out of the truck, walked around to the back, opened the doors, and they shot out of there like they'd been locked in with a lion.

Murch said, "Wha . . ." but there wasn't anybody to ask; they'd all run across the road to the fields on the other side, and though he couldn't see them, the sounds they were making reminded him of clambakes. The endings of clambakes.

Puzzled, he looked into the interior of the truck, but it was too dark to see anything in there. "What the hell," he said, making it a statement because there was nobody around to ask a question of, and walked back up to the cab. In his usual check of the glove compartment he'd seen a flashlight, which he now got and carried back to the rear of the truck. When Dortmunder came stumbling across the road again, Murch was playing the light around the empty inside of the truck and saying, "I don't get it." He looked at Dortmunder. "I give up," he said.

"So do I," said Dortmunder. He looked disgusted. "If I ever tie up with Kelp again, may I be put away. I swear to God."

Now the others were coming back. Herman was saying, "Boy, when you go out to steal a truck, you pick a real winner."

"Is it *my* fault? Can *I* help it? Read the truck for yourself."

"I don't want to read the truck," Herman said. "I never want to *see* the truck again."

"*Read* it," Kelp insisted. He went over and banged the side. "It says *paper!* That's what it *says!*"

"You're gonna wake everybody in the neighborhood," Herman said.

"It says *paper,*" Kelp whispered.

Murch said to Dortmunder quietly, "I don't suppose you're going to tell me about this."

"Ask me tomorrow," Dortmunder said.

Victor came back last, rubbing his face and mouth with a handkerchief. "Wow," he said. "Wow. That was worse than tear gas." He wasn't smiling at all.

Murch shone the flashlight around the inside of the truck one last time, and then shook his head and said, "I don't care. I don't even *want* to know." Still, on the way back up to the cab, he did pause to read the side of the truck, and Kelp had been absolutely right; it said "paper." Murch, looking put-upon, got into the cab again and shut the door behind him. "*Don't* tell me," he muttered.

Meanwhile the other four, also looking put-upon, were getting their gear from inside the truck; they'd traveled light the first time out of it. Herman had a black bag similar to the kind doctors used to carry, back when they made house calls. Dortmunder got his leather jacket and Kelp got his shopping bag.

They all went from the truck over to the fence, where Kelp, looking pained, reached into the shopping bag and pulled out half a dozen cheap steaks, one at a time, and threw them over the fence. The others all faced the other way, and Kelp's nose wrinkled at the smell of food, but he didn't complain. Very quickly after he started throwing the steaks over, they heard the Doberman pinschers arrive on the other side and start snarling among themselves as they gobbled the meat. Murch had counted four of them in his daytime visit here; the other two steaks were just in case he'd missed a couple.

Now Herman carried his black bag over to the broad wooden gate in the fence, hunkered down over the several different locks, opened the bag and went to work. For quite a while, the only sound in the darkness was the tiny clink of Herman's tools.

The idea was, this operation must not exist. The people who worked at Lafferty's Mobile Homes were not to realize tomorrow morning that they'd been burgled tonight. This meant that Dortmunder and the others couldn't just bust through the locks but had to open them in such a way that they would still be usable afterward.

While Herman worked, Dortmunder and Kelp and Victor sat on the ground nearby, their backs against the green wooden fence. Gradually their breathing grew more regular and they got some flesh tone back in their faces. None of them spoke, though once or twice Kelp looked on the verge of a declamation. However, he didn't deliver it.

This part of Long Island, quite a distance out from the city, was semi-rural between the patches of housing developments. The private estates were on the north side; down here, junkyards, car dealers, small assembly plants and Little League baseball diamonds were interspersed amid weedy fields and off-brand gas stations. There were housing developments within a mile of here in three different directions, but no residences in this particular area at all.

"All right," Herman said quietly.

Dortmunder looked along the fence. The gate was hanging slightly open, and Herman was putting his tools away in his black bag. "Okay," Dortmunder said, and he and the others got to their feet. They all went inside and pushed the gate closed behind them.

Murch had made the right count on the dogs; all four of

them were sound asleep, and two of them were snoring. They would wake up in an hour or so with a splitting headache, but the Lafferty's people wouldn't be likely to notice anything tomorrow morning, since dogs like this never do have much by way of a sweet disposition.

The interior of Lafferty's looked like an abandoned city on the moon. If it hadn't been for the big boxes of the mobile homes spaced here and there, it would have been an ordinary junkyard, with its piles of used parts, some mounds of chrome reflecting the dim light and other mounds of grimy dark machinery parts like a wrecked spaceship a thousand years after the crash. But the mobile homes looked almost like houses, with their high walls and their narrow windows and doors, and the way they were canted and leaning here and there around the lot made it look as though this city had been abandoned after an earthquake.

There were floodlights mounted on fairly high poles around and about, but they were so broadly scattered that most of the interior was in a kind of fitful semi-darkness. However, there was enough light to see the paths through the rubble, and Dortmunder had been here with Murch yesterday afternoon, so he knew what spot to head for. The others followed him as he walked straight up the main road, gravel crunching under their feet, and then made a right turn at a pile of chrome window frames and headed straight for a mountain of wheels.

Victor suddenly said, "You know what this is like?" When nobody responded, he answered his own question, saying, "It's like those stories where people suddenly shrink and get very small. And here we are on the toymaker's bench."

Undercarriages. Stacked up higher than their heads, and spreading out sloppily to left and right, were dozens of undercarriages salvaged from defunct mobile homes. Over to the right was another pile of separate wheels, without their tires—to follow Victor's toymaker analogy, the stack of round metal wheels looked like markers in some board game similar to checkers—but it was the complete under-carriages that Dortmunder had in mind. These too were minus tires but were otherwise complete—the two wheels, the axle, the metal framework to attach the whole thing to the bottom of a trailer.

Dortmunder was wearing his leather jacket now, and from the pocket he took a metal tape measure. Murch had given him minimum and maximum dimensions, both in width and height, and Dortmunder started with the easiest undercarriages, the ones off to the side of the main heap.

Most, it turned out, were too small, generally in the way of being too narrow, though Dortmunder did find one good set among those just lying on the ground. Kelp and Herman rolled that one away from the rest, so they could keep track of it, and then all four of them started dismantling the hill of undercarriages, Dortmunder measuring each one as they got it down. The damn things were very heavy, being totally metal, and for the same reason made a lot of noise.

Finally another set came within the usable range of measurements, and that too was set aside. Then they rebuilt the hill—aside from being heavy and loud, the undercarriages were also all dirty and grimy, so that by now all four men were heavily grease-smeared—and when they were done Dortmunder stepped back, panting, and surveyed their work. It looked just about the same as before, the removal of two sets of wheels not changing the appearance of the pile in any significant way.

All that remained now was to roll the undercarriages down to the gate and out. They pushed them along, Dortmunder and Kelp on one and Victor and Herman on the other, and they clattered and banged and made one hell of a lot of noise. It disturbed the dogs, who groaned and moved around in their sleep but didn't quite wake up.

Murch was standing by the open rear of the truck when they came out. He had the flashlight in his hand again, but tucked it away in his jacket pocket when he saw them. "I heard you coming," he said.

They were still rolling the wheels over from the gate to the truck. "What?" shouted Dortmunder, over the racket.

"Forget it," Murch said.

"*What?*"

"Forget it!"

Dortmunder nodded.

They loaded the wheels into the back of the truck, and then Dortmunder said to Murch, "I'll ride up front with you."

"So will I," Herman said very fast.

"We all will," Kelp said, and Victor said, "Darn right."

Murch looked at them all. "You can't fit five people up there," he said.

"We're going to," Dortmunder said.

"It's a *floor* shift."

"Don't worry about it," Kelp said.

Herman said, "We'll manage."

"It's against the law," Murch said. "Two people in the front seat of a floor-shift vehicle, no more. That's the law. What if a cop stops us?"

"Don't worry about it," Dortmunder said. He and the others turned and headed for the cab, leaving Murch to shut the rear doors. Murch did and came around to the left side of the cab to find the other four all jammed into the passenger seat like college students in a phone booth. He shook his head, made no comment, and stepped up behind the wheel.

The only real problem was when he tried to shift into fourth; there seemed to be six or seven knees in that spot. "I have to shift into fourth now," he said, speaking with the even patience of somebody who had decided he isn't going to run amok after all, and a lot of grunting and grumbling took place from the mass beside him as it retracted all its knees, leaving him just enough room to move the shift lever into high.

Fortunately, there weren't many traffic lights on the route he'd worked out, so he didn't have to change gears very often. But the jumble beside him gave a four-throated groan every time they went over a bad bump.

"I am trying to figure out," Murch said conversationally at one point, frowning out the windshield as he spoke, "how this up here can be better than that back there." But he wasn't surprised when no one answered him, and he didn't repeat the remark.

The bankrupt computer-parts factory that Dortmunder and Kelp had found was at last up ahead on the left. Murch drove in there and around to the loading platform at the back, and they all got out again. Herman got his bag of tools from the interior of the truck, unlocked the loading platform door, and by the light of Murch's flashlight they cleared enough space in the rubble for the two sets of wheels. Then Herman locked the place up again.

When it was time to go, they found Murch walking around the interior of the truck, shining his flashlight in the corners. "We're ready," Kelp told him.

Murch frowned at them, all four standing on the loading platform looking in at him. "What's that funny smell?" he said.

"Whiskey," Kelp said.

"Canadian whiskey," Herman said.

Murch gave them a long look. "I see," he said very coldly. He switched off the flashlight, came out onto the platform and shut the rear doors. Then they all got into the cab again, Murch on the left and everybody else on the right, and headed back for where they'd left their cars. Kelp would bring the truck back to where he'd picked it up.

They drove for ten minutes of grunting silence, and then Murch said, "You didn't offer *me* any."

"What?" said the hodgepodge beside him.

"Never mind," Murch said, aiming at a pothole. "It doesn't matter."

15

AT TWENTY after four on Sunday morning, the world still dark with Saturday night, a police patrol car drove slowly past the temporary headquarters of the local branch of the Capitalists' & Immigrants' Trust. The two uniformed patrolmen in the car barely glanced at the trailer containing the bank. Lights were always kept on in there at night and could be seen through the slats of the venetian blinds over all the windows, but the patrolmen knew there was no money inside the trailer, not a dime. They also knew that any burglar who thought there *was* money in there would be sure to trip the alarm when he tried to get in, no matter what method he chose; the alarm would sound down at the station house, and the dispatcher would inform them on their car radio. Since the dispatcher had not so informed them, they knew as they drove by that the C&I Trust trailer was empty, and therefore hardly looked at it at all.

Their confidence was well placed. The entire trailer was wired against burglary. If an amateur were to jimmy open a door or smash the glass in a window, that would naturally sound the alarm, but even a more experienced man would be in trouble if he tried breaking and entering around here. For instance, the entire floor of the trailer was wired; should a man cut a hole in the bottom to come in that way, he too would trip the alarm. Same with the roof and all four walls. A sparrow couldn't have gotten into that mobile home without alerting the people down at the station house.

The patrolmen, as they drove by, paid more attention to the old bank building across the way. There had already been some thievery of building materials from over there, as well as vandalism, though why anybody would want to cause damage to a building that was being torn down anyway was a puzzlement. Still, theirs was not to reason why, so they shone their spotlight over the façade of the old bank building as they passed, saw nothing suspicious or out of the ordinary, and drove on.

Murch let them get a block away and then stepped down from the cab of the truck parked just around the corner on the side street, next to the end of the trailer. Tonight's truck, marked "Hoity Toity Garment Delivery," had been much more thoroughly inspected by Kelp before making delivery, and Murch had by now had last night's conundrums explained to him, so tonight everybody was in a much better mood. Murch, in fact, apologetic for having given the group a bumpier ride home than necessary last night, was going out of his way to be cheerful and helpful.

In the back of the garment delivery truck, in addition to Dortmunder and Kelp and Herman and Victor, were the two sets of wheels for the trailer, now much changed. The boys had spent Saturday afternoon at the defunct computer-parts plant, putting new tires on the wheels and building up the undercarriages with plywood and two-by-fours to get them just the right height. By now they weighed almost twice as much as before and filled most of the interior of the truck.

Murch, having opened the rear doors, said, "The cops just went by. You should have a good half hour now before they come back."

"Right."

It took all five of them to get the wheels down onto the ground and drag them over to the trailer. Dortmunder and Murch unhooked the wooden lattice that closed off the end of the trailer, moved it to one side, and then all five of them shoved and heaved the two sets of wheels into place—one way back near the Kresge's wall, the other up near the front end. Then Murch wrestled the lattice back into position by himself, left it unhooked, and went off to sit in the cab of the truck and keep an eye on things.

Under the trailer, the four of them had taken out pencil flashlights and were looking around for the jacks. There was one jack folded up against the trailer bottom near each corner, and one man to each jack. They were held up there by clips screwed into place, but each man was also equipped with a screwdriver, and it didn't take long to get the things unclipped, fold them down, and crank them till the bottom plates—which looked like duck feet—were placed firmly on the brick rubble underneath. All of this was being done in a space three feet high. It would have been easier if they could have moved around on their knees, but the brick rubble made that impossible, so they waddled around like ducks themselves, in tune with the appearance of the jack plates.

Once they had all whispered back and forth that they were ready, Dortmunder started a rhythmic slow counting, doing one turn on his jack crank with each number: "One . . . two . . . three . . . four . . ." Each of the others turned at the same rhythm, the idea being that the trailer would be lifted straight up, with no canting or angling that might inadvertently set off an alarm. For a long time, though, the trailer didn't lift at all. Nothing happened except that the duck feet crunched deeper and deeper into the brick rubble.

Then, all at once, the bottom of the trailer went *sprong!* It was like an oven cooling and the metal side contracting. They all four of them stopped turning, and while Dortmunder and Victor froze, Herman and Kelp both lost their balance from astonishment and unexpectedly sat down hard on the rubble. "Ow," whispered Kelp, and Herman whispered, "Damn."

They waited half a minute, but nothing else happened, so Dortmunder said softly, "Okay, we'll go on. Twenty-two . . . twenty-three . . . twenty-four . . ."

"It's coming!" Victor whispered excitedly.

It was. All at once illumination from the corner street-light made a thin crack between the bottom of the trailer and the top of the concrete block wall along the front.

"Twenty-five," Dortmunder said. "Twenty-six . . . twenty-seven . . ."

They stopped at forty-two. There was now nearly two inches of air between trailer bottom and concrete block top.

"We'll do the back wheels first," Dortmunder said.

This was difficult. Not because it was complicated but because space was tight and the undercarriage was heavy. A broad metal strip was already mounted beneath the trailer at each end, to take the undercarriages. The strips contained bolt holes, but they hadn't been able to judge ahead of time where to put the corresponding holes in the built-up undercarriages, so now they had first to position each undercarriage and mark the location of the bolt holes and then move the undercarriage—without ramming it too hard or too often into any of the jacks—and place it so Herman could make the holes with a battery-operated drill. Then they put the wheel assembly back against the metal strip, propped it up with extra rubble stuffed under the tires, and put on the bolts and washers and nuts, six bolts to each undercarriage.

It took an hour to get this far, and twice in that time the patrol car ambled by. But they were too busy to notice, and since they were using their flashlights sparingly and shielding the light as much as possible the police also remained unaware of them.

Finally they had the wheels on, and the ground beneath smoothed again, and now they went back to the jacks. When all four of them were ready, they started cranking back down, Dortmunder giving the count again, beginning with "one," not "forty-two."

There was no *sprong* on the way down, and the count ended at thirty-three. They clipped the jacks back into place and restored the screws, and then Dortmunder crawled out from under to check the relationship between the bottom of the trailer and the top of the concrete block wall. They had blown the tires up extra hard, figuring they could let a little air out in order to lower the trailer an inch or so if need be, but as it turned out they didn't have to. The weight of the trailer was enough to use up practically all the leeway they'd left so that there was maybe half an inch at the lattice end of the front wall and practically no space at all down at the Kresge end, where the safe was. Maybe an eighth of an inch.

Dortmunder checked the back, and it was the same there, so he went down to the open end and called softly, "It's okay. Come on out." They'd been waiting in there to be told to let air out of this tire or that.

They came out, Herman carrying his black bag, and while Dortmunder and Victor hooked the lattice back in place Herman and Kelp went around front to finish the job. Herman had a tube of tub caulk, the rubbery stuff that squeezes out soft and never does entirely harden, and while he moved along the wall, squirting this into the crack between the trailer and the concrete blocks, Kelp followed him, smearing dirt onto the caulk to make it blend into the concrete. They did the same thing in the back and then joined the others, who were already in the truck. Murch, who had come out of the cab for the purpose, closed the doors behind them and trotted back up front to drive them away from there.

"Well," Dortmunder said as they all switched on their pencil flashes so they could see one another, "I'd say we did a good night's work."

"By golly!" Victor said excitedly. His eyes sparkled in the lights. "I can hardly wait till Thursday!"

16

JOE MULLIGAN stumbled on his way into the bank and turned to glare at the top step. This was the seventh consecutive Thursday he'd been on this job; you'd think by now he'd know the height of the steps.

"What's the matter, Joe?"

It was Fenton, the senior man. He liked the boys to call him Chief, but none of them ever did. Also, even though they didn't have to be on duty till eight-fifteen, Fenton was always on the job no later than eight o'clock, standing right by the door to see if any of the boys were going to be late. Still, he wasn't such a bad old bird; if you did happen to be late any time, he might give you a word or two on the subject himself, but he wouldn't ever report it to the office.

Mulligan tucked down his dark-blue uniform jacket, readjusted his holster on his right hip, and shook his head. "Getting stumble-footed in my old age," he said.

"Now me, I feel like I got a spring in my step tonight," Fenton said, grinning, and he rocked up onto the balls of his feet for a second to show what he meant.

"I'm glad for you," Mulligan said. As for himself, he would be very pleased—as always on these Thursday nights—when it came around to nine o'clock and the last of the bank employees had gone home and he could sit down and relax. He'd spent a lifetime on his feet and believed there would never be a spring in *his* step again.

He had arrived tonight at eight-fourteen, according to the clock on the wall up behind the tellers. All the other guards were here already except Garfield, who tromped in a minute later—just under the wire—smoothing that Western-marshal mustache of his and looking around as if he hadn't decided for sure whether to guard the bank or hold it up.

Mulligan had by this time taken up his usual Thursday-evening post, against the wall near the pretty girl at the courtesy desk outside the counter. He'd always been partial to pretty girls. He was also partial to her chair and liked to be the nearest one to it.

The bank was still open and would be until eight-thirty, so for the next fifteen minutes it would be very crowded, what with its normal complement of employees and customers added to by the seven private guards, Mulligan and the other six. All seven wore the same police-officerlike uniform, with the triangular badge on the left shoulder reading *Continental Detective Agency*. Their shields, embossed with CDA and their number, were also policelike, and so were their gun belts and holsters and the .38-caliber Smith & Wesson Police Positive revolvers within them. Most of them, including Mulligan, had been police officers at one time and had no trouble looking natural in the uniform. Mulligan had been on the force in New York City for twelve years but hadn't liked the way things were going and had spent the last nine years with Continental. Garfield had been an MP, and Fenton had spent twenty-five years as a cop in some city in Massachusetts, retired on half pay, and was working for Continental now as much to keep himself occupied as to augment his income. Fenton was the only one with any additional insignia on his uniform; the two blue chevrons on his sleeves meant he was a sergeant. The CDA had only the two uniformed ranks, guard and sergeant, and used sergeants only where a job called for more than three men. They also had an Operative classification, which was for plainclothes work, a job toward which Mulligan did not aspire. He knew that being a Continental Op was supposed to be glamorous, but he was a flatfoot, not a detective, and content to remain so.

At eight-thirty the regular bank guard, an old man named Nieheimer, not a CDA man, locked both bank doors and then stood by one of them to keep unlocking it again for the next five minutes or so, letting the last customers out. Then the employees did their closing paperwork, put all the cash away in the safe, covered the typewriters and adding machines, and by nine o'clock the last of them—that was always Kingworthy, the manager—was ready to go home. Fenton always stood by the door to watch Kingworthy out and be sure the manager locked up properly on the outside. The way the system worked, the alarm could be switched on or off only with a key on the outside; once Kingworthy left, the guards inside couldn't open either door without sounding the alarm down at police headquarters. For that reason, all seven guards brought lunch bags or lunch buckets. There was also a men's room at the front end of the trailer, the end farthest from the safe.

Nine o'clock. Kingworthy left, he locked up, Fenton

turned and said what he said every Thursday night: "Now we're on duty."

"Right," Mulligan said and reached for the courtesy desk's chair. Meanwhile, Block was going down to get the folding table from where it was stored by the safe, and the others were all heading for their favorite chairs. Within a minute, the folding table was set up in the customer area of the bank, the seven guards were in seven chairs around it, and Morrison had pulled the two fresh decks from his uniform pocket—one deck with blue backs, the other with red—and they were all taking handfuls of change from their pockets and slapping them down on the table.

Seven cards were dealt around, with the high card to be the first dealer, and that turned out to be Dresner. "Five-card stud," he said, put a nickel in the pot and started to deal.

Mulligan was sitting with his back to the safe, facing the front of the trailer; that is, the part with the officers' desks. The tellers' counter was to his right, the two locked doors to his left. He sat with his legs spread wide, both feet flat on the floor, and watched Dresner deal him a five of hearts up. He looked at his hole card, and it was the two of spades. Morrison bet a nickel—it was nickel limit on the first card, dime after that, twenty cents on the last—and when it came around to Mulligan he very quietly folded. "I don't believe this is going to be my night," he said.

It wasn't. By one-thirty in the morning he was losing four dollars and seventy cents. However, Fox occasionally dealt draw poker, jacks or better to open, and at one-thirty he did it again. In draw, each player anted at the beginning, so they started off with a thirty-five-cent pot. When no one could open and Fox had to deal out another hand, they all anted again. Still no one could open, and when Mulligan looked at his third hand and saw three sixes in it there was already a dollar-five in the pot. To top it off, Fenton on his right opened, with a quarter, the maximum bid. Mulligan thought of raising, but decided to keep as many players in as possible, so just called. So did Garfield and Block. Two dollars and five cents in the pot now.

It was time for the draw. Fenton, the opener, took three

new cards; so he had only the one high pair, jacks or over, to begin with. Mulligan considered; if he took two cards, they'd all suspect he had trips. But he was known to be a man to try for straights and flushes, so if he took only one card they'd think he was at it again. In addition to the three sixes, he had a queen and a four; he threw away the four and said, "One card."

Garfield chuckled. "Still trying, eh, Joe?"

"I guess so," Mulligan said and looked at another queen.

"An honest three," Garfield said. So he, too, was starting with only a pair—probably aces or kings, hoping to just beat out Fenton's openers.

"A dishonest one," Block said. Which was either two pair, or an attempt to buy a flush or a straight.

After the draw, the maximum bet was fifty cents, and that's what Fenton bet. So he'd improved.

Mulligan looked at his cards, though he hadn't forgotten them. Three sixes and two queens—a very nice full house. "I believe I'll just raise," he said and plucked a dollar bill from his shirt pocket and dropped it casually among the coins in the pot.

Now there was three fifty-five in the pot. Mulligan had put in a dollar-forty, meaning he could win two dollars and fifteen cents if nobody called his raise.

Garfield frowned at his cards. "I'm kind of sorry I bought," he said. "I'm just gonna have to call you, Joe." And put in his own dollar.

"And I'm just gonna have to raise," Block said. He put in a dollar and a half.

"Well, now," Fenton said. "I bought a second little pair, but I suddenly don't believe they'll win. I fold."

The pot now had four dollars and sixty-five cents in it that Mulligan hadn't put in there. If he just called—and if he won—he would be within a nickel of breaking even on the night. If he lost, he would be down another two dollars and forty cents, all in one hand.

"The hand of the night," Morrison said disgustedly, "and I'm not in it."

"I'd just about trade places with you," Mulligan said. He

kept staring at his hand and thinking. If he actually raised another half dollar, and got even one call, and won, he'd be ahead on the night. On the other hand . . .

Well, what did those two have? Garfield had started with a high pair and had taken three cards and improved—meaning more than likely either triplets or a second pair. In either case, nothing to worry about. Block, on the other hand, had taken only one card. If he'd been buying to a straight or flush, and if he'd bought, Mulligan's full house would beat him. But what if Block had started with two pair and had bought a full house of his own? Mulligan's full house was based on sixes; that left a lot of higher numbers for Block to come up with.

Garfield, sounding nervous and irritated, said, "Are you going to make up your mind?"

It was, as Morrison had said, the hand of the night. So he ought to play it that way. "I'll raise half a dollar," he said.

"Fold," Garfield said in prompt disgust.

"Raise you right back again," Block said, dropped a dollar in the pot, and smiled like the cat that ate the canary.

A higher full house. Mulligan was suddenly very depressed. It couldn't be anything else; it had to be a higher full house. But he'd come this far . . . "I'll call," Mulligan said wearily and shoved in yet another half dollar.

"King high flush," Block said, spreading the cards out. "All diamonds."

"By *God!*" Mulligan cried and lifted his hand over his head to slap it down in the middle of the table with the full house showing; but just as his arm reached the top of its swing, he was suddenly jerked backward, up over the chair and onto the suddenly bouncing floor. And as he went flailing back, his legs kicked up into the under part of the table and sent it too flying; nickels and dimes and cards and guards exploded in all directions, and a second later the lights went out.

17

AT THIS HOUR on a Thursday night there were three police dispatchers on duty down at the station house. They sat in a row at a long continuous table, each one equipped with three telephones and a two-way radio, all three facing a big square panel of lights built into the opposite wall. The panel was four feet on a side, edged with a wooden frame, and looked like the kind of thing hung in the Museum of Modern Art. Against a flat black background, sixteen rows of sixteen frosted red bulbs stuck out, each with a number painted on it in white. At the moment none of the bulbs were lit, and the composition might have been titled "Tail Lights at Rest."

At 1:37 A.M. a tail light lit up—number fifty-two. At the same time, a very annoying buzzing sound started, as though it were time to get out of bed.

The dispatchers worked in strict sequence, to avoid confusion, and this squeal—which was what the fuzz called the buzz—was the property of the man on the left, who pushed a button that stopped the noise, at the same time saying, "Mine." Then, while his left hand reached for one of the phones and his right hand switched the radio to *send,* he quickly glanced at the typewritten list on the table in front of him, under a piece of glass, and saw that number fifty-two was the temporary branch of Capitalists' & Immigrants' Trust.

"Car nine," he said, while with his left hand, still holding the phone receiver, he dialed the number *seven,* which was the captain's office, currently occupied by the senior man on duty, Lieutenant Hepplewhite.

Car nine was the regular patrol car past the bank, and

tonight the men on duty were Officers Bolt and Echer. Bolt was driving, very slowly, and had driven past the bank just five minutes ago, not long before Joe Mulligan was dealt his three sixes.

Echer, the passenger right now, was the one who answered the call, unhooking the mike from under the dashboard, depressing the button in its side, saying, "Car nine here."

"Alarm at C and I bank, Floral Avenue and Tenzing Street."

"Which one?"

"It's on the corner of both of them."

"Which *bank*."

"Oh. The temporary one, the new one, the temporary one."

"That one, huh?"

Ambling, it had taken five minutes to come this far from the bank. Flat out, siren screaming, red light flashing, it took less than two minutes to get back. In that time, Lieutenant Hepplewhite had been informed and had alerted the men downstairs on standby, who were playing poker as it happened, though nobody had had a full house all night. "The colds are card," Officer Kretschmann said in disgust at one point, and the others hardly even noticed; he did that kind of thing all the time.

Two other patrol cars, on beats farther away, had also been alerted and were rushing toward the scene. (The standby men alerted at the station house were not as yet rushing toward the scene, though they had stopped playing poker and had put on their jackets and guns; having been alerted, they were standing by.) The dispatcher who had handled the squeal was staying with it, answering no other calls until car nine should report.

"Uhhhh," said the radio. "Dispatcher?"

"Is this car nine?"

"This is car nine. It isn't here."

The dispatcher felt a sudden instant of panic. The trouble wasn't there? He looked again at the red light, which was still lit even though the buzzer was off, and it was number fifty-two. He looked at his typewritten sheet, and fifty-two was the temporary bank. "Well, it *was* there," he said.

"I know it *was* here," said car nine. "I saw it only five minutes ago. But it isn't here now."

The dispatcher was by now completely bewildered. "You saw it five minutes ago?"

"Last time we went by."

"Now wait a minute," the dispatcher said. His voice was rising, and the other two dispatchers looked at him oddly. A dispatcher was supposed to stay calm. "Wait a minute," the dispatcher repeated. "You knew about this trouble five *minutes* ago and you didn't *report* it?"

"No no no," car nine said, and another voice behind it said, "Let *me* have that." Then it apparently took over the microphone, becoming louder when it said, "Dispatcher, this is Officer Bolt. We are at the scene, and the bank is gone."

There was silence from the dispatcher for several seconds. On the scene, Officer Bolt stood next to the patrol car, holding the microphone to his mouth. He and Officer Echer both gazed at the place where the bank had been—Officer Echer in a glazed manner, Officer Bolt in an aggravated and brooding manner.

The low concrete block walls were there, but above them was nothing but space. Wind blew through the air where the bank had been; if you squinted, you could almost see the structure standing there, as though it had become invisible but was still present.

To left and right, wires dangled like hair from the telephone and power poles. Two sets of wooden steps led up to the top of the concrete block wall and stopped.

The dispatcher, his voice nearly as thin as the air where the bank had been, finally said, "The bank is gone?"

"That's right," Officer Bolt said, nodding in irritation. From far away he could hear more sirens coming. "Some son of a bitch," he said, "has stole the bank."

18

INSIDE the bank, everything was chaos and confusion. Dortmunder and the others hadn't bothered about springs, shock absorbers, none of the luxuries; wheels had been their only concern. Since they were now moving pretty fast, the result was that the bank dipped and swooped and bounced pretty much like a kite at the end of a string.

"I had a full house!" Joe Mulligan wailed in the darkness. Every time he managed to get to his feet some chair or some other guard would come bowling along and knock him over again, so now he was just staying down, hunkering on hands and knees and bawling his announcement into the darkness. "You hear me? I had a full house!"

From somewhere in the confusion—it was like being in an avalanche in an aquarium—Block's voice answered: "For Christ's sake, Joe, that hand is dead!"

"Sixes full! I had sixes full!"

Fenton, who had been quiet till now, suddenly shouted, "Forget poker! Don't you realize what's happening? Somebody's stealing the bank!"

Until that moment, Mulligan actually *hadn't* realized what was happening.

With his mind occupied on the one hand by his full house and on the other hand by the difficulty of simply keeping his balance in this jouncing darkness and not getting beaned by a passing chair, it hadn't until just that instant occurred to Mulligan that this disaster was anything more than his own personal disaster at poker.

Which he couldn't very well admit, particularly not to Fenton, so he shouted back, "Of *course* I realize some stealing the bank!" And then he heard the words he'd just said and spoiled the effect by squeaking, "Stealing the *bank?*"

"We need light in here!" Dresner shouted. "Who's got a flashlight?"

"Get them venetian blinds up!" Morrison yelled.

"I have a flashlight!" Garfield shouted, and a spot of white light showed, though the confusion it revealed wasn't much more informative than darkness. Then the light swooped down and away, and Garfield shouted, "I dropped the goddam thing!" Mulligan watched its progression, the bouncing white light, and if there'd been words under it they could have sung along. It seemed to be headed his way, and he braced himself to make a grab for it, but before it got to him it suddenly disappeared. Went out, or something.

However, a few seconds later somebody at last got a venetian blind opened, and it was possible at last to see, in the illumination of streetlights whipping by outside. Intervals of darkness and light succeeded one another at great speed, like a flickering silent movie, but it gave light enough for Mulligan to crawl on all fours through the scattered furniture and sprawled guards and rolling nickels over to the tellers' counter. He crawled up that and thus reached his feet. Feet braced wide, both arms stretched out across the counter and fingers gripping the inner edge, he looked around at the shambles.

Down to his left, Fenton was also clinging to the counter, in the angle where it made a turn to go past the courtesy desk. Sitting on the floor with his back to the courtesy desk and his hands braced to both sides was Morrison, wincing at every bump. Across the way, clutching the neck-high windowsill where the venetian blind was up, hung Dresner, trying to make some sense out of the night scenes flashing past the window.

What about the other direction? Block and Garfield were in a tight embrace in the corner where the counter—with the safe past it—met the wall of the trailer; sitting there, locked together, half buried under furniture and debris since the general trend of everything loose was to head toward the rear of the trailer, they looked mostly like a high-school couple on a hayride.

And where was Fox? Fenton must have wondered the same thing, because he suddenly yelled, "Fox! Where'd you get to!"

"I'm here!"

It was Fox's voice all right, but where was Fox? Mulligan gaped around, and so did everybody else.

And then Fox appeared. His head emerged above the counter, down by the safe. He was on *the other side* of the counter. Hanging there, he looked seasick. "Here I am," he called.

Fenton saw him, too, since he yelled, "How in God's name did you get in *there?*"

"I just don't know," Fox said. "I just don't know."

Block and Garfield were now coming back toward the middle space, both traveling on all fours. They looked like fathers who didn't yet realize their sons had grown bored with piggyback and gone away. Garfield paused in front of Fenton, hunkered back, looked up like the dog on the old Victrola record labels, and said, "Shall we try to break out the door?"

"What, leave?" Fenton looked enraged, as though somebody had suggested they surrender the fort to the Indians. "They may have the bank," he said, "but they don't have the money!" He let go with one arm to gesture dramatically at the safe. Unfortunately, the bank made a right turn at the same instant and Fenton suddenly ran across the floor and tackled Dresner, over at the window. The two of them went crashing, and Block and Garfield rolled into them.

Turning his head to the left, Mulligan, who had retained his grip on the counter, saw Morrison still sitting on the floor against the courtesy desk and still wincing. Turning his head to the right, he saw that Fox's head was no longer on top of the counter, nor anywhere else in view. He nodded, having expected as much.

From the scramble across the way, Fenton's voice rose: "Get off me, you men! Get off me, I say! That's a direct order!"

Mulligan, his chest against the counter, looked over his shoulder at the rest.

An awful lot of legs were flailing over there, and they still hadn't sorted themselves out when suddenly the flickering light stopped, and they were in darkness again.

"Now what?" Fenton wailed, his voice muffled as though somebody possibly had their elbow in his mouth.

"We're not in the city any more," Morrison shouted. "We're in the country. No streetlights."

"Get *off* me!"

For some reason it all seemed quieter in the dark, though just as jouncy and chaotic. Mulligan clung to the counter like Ishmael, and in the darkness they eventually sorted themselves out across the way. Finally Fenton, panting, said, "All right. Everybody present?" He then called the role, and each of the six pantingly answered to his name—even Fox, though faintly.

"All right," Fenton said again. "Sooner or later they're going to have to stop. They're going to want to get in here. Now, they may shoot the place up first, so what we have to do is all of us get in back of that counter. Try to keep a desk or some other piece of furniture between you and any outside wall. They have the bank, but they don't have the money, and as long as we're on the job they aren't going to get the money!"

It might have been an inspiring speech if it hadn't been slowed down by all the panting Fenton was doing, and if the rest of them hadn't had to hold onto the walls and one another for dear life while listening to it. Still, it did recall them all to their duties, and Mulligan heard them now crawling toward the counter, panting and bumping into things, but making progress.

Mulligan had to go by his memory of the place, since he couldn't see his hand in front of his face. Or wouldn't have been able to if it was there and not clutching the counter. As he remembered the layout, the nearest entrance through the counter was down to his right, toward the safe. He moved that way, sidling along, keeping both hands firmly on the counter edge.

He too was panting, which he could surely understand,

given the exertion required simply to keep on his feet, but why should he be so sleepy? He'd been working a night shift for years; he hadn't gotten out of bed yesterday until four in the afternoon. It was ridiculous to feel sleepy. Nevertheless, it would feel very good to sit down, once he got around behind this counter. Wedge himself in next to a filing cabinet or something, relax a little. Not actually close his eyes, of course—just relax.

19

"CALLING all cars, calling all cars. Be on the lookout for a stolen bank, approximately eleven feet tall, blue and white . . ."

20

DORTMUNDER, Kelp and Murch were the only gang members present at the actual theft of the bank. Kelp, earlier that evening, had picked up a tractor-trailer cab without its trailer near the piers in the West Village section of Manhattan and had met Dortmunder and Murch with it on Queens Boulevard in Long Island City, just across the 59th Street bridge from Manhattan, shortly after midnight.

Murch had done the driving after that, with Kelp sitting in the middle and Dortmunder on the right, resting his elbow on the open windowsill. Below his elbow read a company name: Elmore Trucking. The cab had North Dakota plates. Stuffed inside with them, amid their feet as they headed east out Long Island, were a twenty-five-foot coil of black rubber garden hose, several lengths of thick heavy chain and a carpenter's tool kit.

They arrived at the bank at one-fifteen and had to move a car parked in the way. They pushed it down in front of a fire hydrant and took its place and waited silently with the lights and engine off until they saw the patrol car—car nine—drive by just after one-thirty. Very quietly then they backed the cab up to the trailer and left its engine idling but lights off while they hooked the two parts together.

Which was a little complicated. The tractor cab was of the sort that fits under the front of a cargo-carrying trailer equipped only with rear wheels; that is, the cab's rear wheels normally served as the front wheels of any trailer it towed, with the front section of the trailer resting on the low flat rear section of the cab. But this particular trailer, the bank, being a mobile home instead of a cargo transporter, wasn't set up for that kind of rig, having instead a kind of modified V hitch in front, which was supposed to lock onto a ball at the rear of the towing vehicle. So Dortmunder and Kelp and Murch had to attach the two together with the loops of chain, shushing each other at every rattle and clank, squeezing links shut with the pliers from the tool kit in order to complete the loops and attach trailer to cab with four heavy circles of chain.

One end of the garden hose was then stuck into the cab's tailpipe, and while Kelp wrapped lots of black tape around the hose and that end of the pipe Dortmunder stood on the rear of the cab and shoved the other end through an air vent high in the trailer wall, so the cab exhaust would now go into the bank. More tape was used to fasten that end of the hose in place, and to keep the length of it flat against the front of the trailer all the way down, and to attach the extra coils of hose to the rear superstructure of the cab.

All of which had taken only three or four minutes. Murch and Kelp got back into the cab, Kelp carrying the tool kit, and Dortmunder made one last check before trotting around and swinging up into the cab on the right side. "Set," he said.

"I'm not gonna start slow," Murch said. "We're gonna have to jerk it loose and then go like hell. So hold on."

"Any time," Kelp said.

"Now," Murch said, threw it in first, and jumped on the accelerator with both feet.

The cab lunged forward like a dog that had backed into a hot stove. There was a grinding noise that none of them heard over the engine roar, and the bank snapped its moorings—these being the water pipe in and the sewage pipe out of the bathroom. As water spurted up from the broken city water pipe like Old Faithful geyser, the bank slid away leftward over its concrete wall, like a name card being slipped out of a slot in a door. Murch, not wanting to turn before the bank's rear wheels had cleared the concrete blocks, tore straight ahead across the side street, began to spin the steering wheel only as his front tires thumped up over the curb on the other side, and as Kelp and Dortmunder both yelled and waved their arms he angled the cab leftward so it just missed the bakery windows on the corner, drove catty-corner across the sidewalk at the intersection, thumped down off the curb again on the other side, shot out across the main street at a long angle, straightened out at last on the wrong side of the street, and took off.

Behind them, the left rear wheel of the bank had just nicked the edge of the concrete block wall, but aside from an extra jounce it caused no obvious damage, though it did loosen a couple of the screws holding the rear wheels to the bottom of the trailer. The bank followed the cab, thumping and bumping up and down over curbs, missing the bakery windows by even less than the cab because it was so much wider, and shuddered and rocked from side to side as it swept on away down the street in the cab's wake. An automatic cutoff valve had already shut down the water from the main line into this spur, and the geyser had stopped.

Murch had planned his route with the greatest care. He knew which secondary streets were wide enough to allow the bank passage, which major streets could be traveled for brief periods without the likelihood of running into traffic. He made left turns and right turns with a minimum use of brakes or lower gears, and behind him the bank rocked and reeled and occasionally took corners on two wheels but never did go over. The greatest weight in the thing was the safe, which was at the back, which gave it more stability the faster Murch drove.

Kelp and Dortmunder and the tool kit, meanwhile, were all over each other. Dortmunder surfaced at last to shout, *"Are they on our tail?"*

Murch gave a quick look to the outside mirror. "Nobody back there at all," he said, and took a left turn so hard it popped the glove-compartment door open and a package of No-Doz dropped into Kelp's lap. Kelp picked it up in trembling fingers and said, "Never did I need you less."

"Then slow down!" Dortmunder yelled.

"Nothing to worry about," Murch said. His headlights showed a pair of cars parked up ahead, opposite each other, both too far out from the curb, leaving a space that was under the circumstances very small. "Everything under control," Murch said, jiggled the wheels as he went through, and simply amputated the outside mirror from the car on the right.

"Uh," said Kelp. He dropped the No-Doz on the floor and shut the glove compartment.

Dortmunder looked past Kelp at Murch's profile, saw how absorbed it was, and understood there was no way right now to attract Murch's attention without actually setting up a roadblock ahead of him. And that might not do it, either. "I trust you," Dortmunder said, since he had no choice, and sat back in the corner to brace himself and to watch the night thunder at their windshield.

They drove for twenty minutes, mostly heading north, sometimes heading east. Generally speaking, the south shore of Long Island, which faces the Atlantic Ocean, is less prestigious than the north shore, which faces Long Island Sound, a mostly enclosed body of water protected by the island on one side and Connecticut on the other. In taking the bank from the south-shore community it had serviced so well, and in heading north with it, Murch and Dortmunder and Kelp were moving by gradual stages from smaller older houses on narrower plots of land to larger newer houses on broader plots of land. Similarly, westward, toward New York City, the houses were poorer and closer together, but eastward they were richer and farther apart. In going both east and north, Murch was giving this branch of the C&I Trust a literal kind of upward mobility.

They were also moving into an area where there was still undeveloped land between the towns, rather than the undifferentiated sweep of suburb that characterized the section where they'd started. After twenty minutes, they had crossed a county line and were on a deserted bit of cracked and bumpy two-lane road, with a farmer's field on the right and a stand of trees on the left. "This is close enough," Murch said, and began tapping the brake. "God damn it," he said.

Dortmunder sat up. "What's the matter? Brakes no good?"

"Brakes are fine," Murch said through clenched teeth, and tapped them some more. "Goddam bank wants to jackknife," he said.

Dortmunder and Kelp twisted around to look through the small rear window at the bank. Every time Murch touched the brakes, the trailer began to slue around, the rear of it moving leftward like a car in a skid on ice. Kelp said, "It looks like it wants to pass us."

"It does," Murch said. He kept tapping, and very gradually they slowed, and when they got below twenty miles an hour Murch could apply the brakes more normally and bring them to a stop. "Son of a bitch," he said. His hands were still clawed around the wheel, and sweat was running down his cheeks from his forehead.

Kelp said, "Were we really in trouble, Stan?"

"Well, I'll tell you," Murch said, breathing slowly but

heavily. "I just kept wishing Christopher was still a saint."

"Let's go take a look at things," Dortmunder said. What he meant was that he wanted to go stand on the ground for a minute.

So did the others. All three got out and wasted several seconds just stomping their feet on the cracked pavement. Then Dortmunder took a revolver from his jacket pocket and said, "Let's see how it worked out."

"Right," Kelp said, and from his own pocket took a key ring containing a dozen keys. Herman had assured him that one of those keys would definitely open the bank door. "At least one," he'd said. "Maybe even more than one." But Kelp had said, "One will do."

So it did. It was the fifth key he tried, while Murch stood back a few feet with a flashlight, and then the door swung outward. Kelp stayed behind it, because they weren't sure about the guards inside, whether the carbon-monoxide truck exhaust had knocked them out or not. They had made careful calculations on how much of the cubic-foot capacity the gas would fill after x minutes and $x + y$ minutes, and were certain they were well within safety limits. So Dortmunder called, "Come out with your hands up."

Kelp said, "The robbers aren't supposed to say that to the cops. The cops are supposed to say it to the robbers."

Dortmunder ignored him. "Come out," he called again. "Don't make us drill you."

There was no response.

"Flashlight," Dortmunder said quietly, like a doctor asking for a scalpel, and Murch handed it to him. Dortmunder moved cautiously forward, pressed himself against the wall of the trailer, and slowly looked around the edge of the door frame. Both his hands were in front of himself, pointing the gun and the flashlight at the same spot.

There was no one in sight. Furniture lay scattered all over the place, and the floor was littered with credit-card applications, small change and playing cards. Dortmunder waggled the flashlight around, continued to see no one, and said, "That's funny."

Kelp said, "What's funny?"

"There's nobody there."

"You mean we stole an empty bank?"

"The question is," Dortmunder said, "did we steal an empty safe."

"Oh oh," Kelp said.

"I should have known," Dortmunder said, "the first second I saw you. And if not you, when I saw your nephew."

"Let's at least look it over," Kelp said.

"Sure. Give me a boost."

All three of them climbed up into the bank and began to look around, and it was Murch who found the guards. "Here they are," he said. "Behind the counter."

And there they were, all seven of them, stuffed away on the floor behind the counter, jammed in amid filing cabinets and desks, sound asleep. Murch said, "I heard that one snoring, that's how I knew."

"Don't they look peaceful," Kelp said, looking over the counter at them. "It makes me woozy myself just to look at them."

Dortmunder too had been feeling a certain heaviness, thinking it was the physical and emotional letdown after a successful job, but all at once he roused himself and cried, "Murch!"

Murch was half draped over the counter; it was hard to tell if he was looking at the guards or joining them. He straightened, startled by Dortmunder's shout, and said, "What? What?"

"Is the motor still on?"

"My God, so it is," Murch said. He reeled toward the door. "I'll go turn it off."

"No no," Dortmunder said. "Just get that damn hose out of the ventilator." He gestured with the flashlight toward the front of the trailer, where the hose had been pumping truck exhaust into the trailer for the last twenty minutes. There was a strong smell of garage inside the bank, but it hadn't been enough to warn them right away not to fall into their own trap. The guards had been put to sleep by carbon monoxide, and their captors had almost just done the same thing to themselves.

Murch staggered out into the fresh air, and Dortmunder said to Kelp, who was yawning like a whale, "Come on, let's get these birds out of here."

"Right, right, right." Knuckling his eyes, Kelp followed Dortmunder around the counter, and they spent the next few minutes carrying guards outside and depositing them in the grass by the side of the road. When they were finished with that, they hooked the door open, propped the trailer windows open, and got back into the cab, where they found Murch asleep.

"Oh, come on," Dortmunder said, and joggled Murch's shoulder hard enough to bump his head into the door.

"Ow," Murch said and looked around, blinking. "What now?" he said, obviously trying to remember what situation he was in.

"Onward," Kelp said.

"Right," Dortmunder said and slammed the cab door.

21

AT FIVE past two, Murch's Mom said, "I hear them coming!" and raced to the car for her neck brace. She barely had it on and fastened when the headlights appeared at the end of the stadium, and the cab and bank drove across the football field and stopped on the drop cloth. Meanwhile, Herman and Victor and May were standing by with their equipment ready. This high-school football stadium was open and untenanted. The stands on three sides, and the school building beyond the open side, shielded them from curious eyes on any of the neighborhood roads.

Murch had barely stopped the cab when Victor was setting up the ladder at the back and Herman was climbing the ladder with his roller in one hand and paint tray in the other. Meanwhile, May and Murch's Mom had started, with newspapers and masking tape, to cover all sections on the sides that wouldn't get painted—windows, chrome trim, door handles.

There were more rollers and ladders and paint trays. While Victor and Murch helped the ladies mask the sides, Kelp and Dortmunder started painting. They were using a pale-green water-base paint, the kind people use on their living-room walls, the kind you can clean up afterward with plain water. They were using this because it was the fastest and neatest to apply, it was guaranteed to cover in one coat, and it would dry very quickly. Particularly in the open air.

In five minutes, the bank wasn't a bank any more. It had lost its "Just watch us GROW!" sign somewhere along the way and was now a pleasing soft green color instead of its former blue and white. It had also gained Michigan license plates appropriate to a mobile home. Murch drove forward till it was off the drop cloth, and then the drop cloth was folded up and put into the paint-company truck that had been stolen this afternoon for just this purpose. The ladders and rollers and paint trays were stowed away in there, too. Then Herman and May and Dortmunder and Murch's Mom climbed up into the trailer, the ladies both carrying packages, and Kelp drove away in the paint-company truck, followed by Victor in the Packard. Victor had brought the ladies out here and would take Kelp home after he ditched the truck.

Murch, alone in the cab now, made a sweeping U-turn and drove out of the football field. He drove more slowly and carefully now, both because the urgency was gone and because his Mom and some other people were in the back.

What they were doing in the back, May was putting up on the windows the curtains she'd been making all week. Murch's Mom was holding the two flashlights that were their only illumination, and Dortmunder was cleaning up the mess a bit while Herman was squatting on the floor in front of the safe, looking it over and saying, "Hmmmmm." He didn't look pleased.

22

"A BANK doesn't just disappear," Captain Deemer said.

"Yes, sir," said Lieutenant Hepplewhite.

Captain Deemer extended his arms out at the sides as though he would do calisthenics and wiggled his hands. "It doesn't just fly away," he said.

"No, sir," said Lieutenant Hepplewhite.

"So we have to be able to *find* it, Lieutenant."

"Yes, sir."

They were alone in the captain's office, a small and deceptively quiet life raft in a sea of chaos—the eye of the storm, as it were. Beyond that door, men were running back and forth, scribbling messages, slamming doors, making phone calls, developing heartburn and acid indigestion. Beyond that window, a massive bank hunt was already under way, with every available car and man from both the Nassau County police *and* the Suffolk County police. The New York City police in both Queens and Brooklyn had been alerted, and every street and road and highway crossing the twelve-mile-long border into the city was being watched. There was no land exit from Long Island except through New York City, no bridges or tunnels to any other part of the world. The ferries to Connecticut from Port Jefferson and Orient Point didn't run at this time of night and would be watched from the time they opened for business in the morning. The local police and harbor authorities at every spot on the Island with facilities big enough to handle a ship that could load an entire mobile home on it had also been alerted and were ready. MacArthur Airport was being watched.

"We have them bottled up," Captain Deemer said grimly, bringing his hands slowly together as though to strangle somebody.

"Yes, sir," said Lieutenant Hepplewhite.

"Now all we have to do is *tighten the net!*" And Captain Deemer squeezed his hands shut and twisted them together, as though snapping the neck off a chicken.

Lieutenant Hepplewhite winced. "Yes, sir," he said.

"And get those sons of bitches," Captain Deemer said, shaking his head from side to side, "that woke me up out of bed."

"Yes, sir," Lieutenant Hepplewhite said and flashed a sickly grin.

Because it had been Lieutenant Hepplewhite who had awakened Captain Deemer out of his bed. It had been the only thing to do, the proper thing to do, and the lieutenant knew the captain didn't blame him personally for it, but nevertheless the act had made Lieutenant Hepplewhite very nervous, and nothing that had happened since had served to calm him down.

The lieutenant and the captain were different in almost every respect—the lieutenant young, slender, hesitant, quiet and a reader, the captain fiftyish, heavyset, bullheaded, loud and illiterate—but they did have one trait they shared in common: Neither of them liked trouble. It was the one area in which they even used the same language: "I want things *quiet,* men," the captain would tell his men at the morning shape-up, and at the night shape-up the lieutenant would say, "Let's keep things *quiet,* men, so I don't have to wake the captain." They were both death on police corruption, because it might tend to endanger the quiet.

If they'd wanted noise, after all, New York City was right next door, and its police force was always looking for recruits.

But it was noise they had tonight, whether they liked it or not. Captain Deemer turned away from the lieutenant, muttering, "It's just a goddam good thing I was home," and went over to brood at the map of the Island on the side wall.

"Sir?"

"Never mind, Lieutenant," said the captain.

"Yes, sir."

The phone rang.

"Get that, Lieutenant."

"Yes, sir."

Hepplewhite spoke briefly into the phone—he stood beside the desk, not wanting to sit at it in the captain's presence—and then put the caller on hold and said, "Captain, the people from the bank are here."

"Have 'em come in." The captain kept brooding at the map, and his lips moved without sound. "Tighten the net," he seemed to be saying.

The three men who entered the office looked like some sort of statistical sampling, a cross-section of America perhaps; the mind boggled at the attempt to see them as a group connected with one another.

The first in was portly, distinguished, with iron-gray hair and black suit and conservative narrow tie. He carried a black attaché case, and fat cigar tips protruded from his breast pocket. He looked to be about fifty-five, prosperous, and used to giving orders.

The second was stocky, short, wearing a tan sports jacket, dark-brown slacks and a bow tie. He had crewcut sandy hair, horn-rimmed glasses, leather patches on the elbows of his jacket, and carried a brown briefcase. He was about forty and looked thoughtful and competent in some specialty.

The third was very tall and very thin, with shoulder-length hair, deep sideburns and Western-sheriff mustache. He was no more than twenty-five and wore a yellow pullover polo shirt, tie-dye blue jeans and white basketball sneakers. He carried a gray cloth bag of the kind plumbers use, which clanked when he put it down on a chair. He grinned all the time and did a lot of bobbing in place, as though listening to music.

The portly man looked around with a tentative smile. "Captain Deemer?"

The captain remained by the map but looked over with brooding eyes and said, "That's me."

"I am George Gelding, of C and I."

The captain gave an irritated frown. "Seeing-eye?"

"Capitalists' and Immigrants' Trust," said Gelding. "The bank you lost."

The captain grunted, as though he'd been hit in the chest with an arrow, and lowered his head like a bull deciding to get mad.

Gelding gestured to the man with the bow tie and leather elbow patches. "This is Mr. Albert Docent," he said, "of the company which provided the safe employed in that particular branch of our bank."

Deemer and Docent nodded at each other, the captain sourly, the safe man with a thoughtful smile.

"And this," Gelding said, gesturing to the young man with the hair, "is Mr. Gary Wallah, of Roamerica Corporation, the company which provided the trailer in which the bank has recently been housed."

"Mobile home," Wallah said. He grinned and nodded and bounced.

"Mobile, at any rate," Gelding said and turned back to the captain, saying, "We are here to offer you whatever information and expertise may be of help to you."

"Thank you."

"And to ask if there have been any further developments."

"We have them bottled up," the captain said grimly.

"Have you really?" said Gelding, smiling broadly and taking a step forward. "Where?"

"Here," the captain said and thumped the map with the back of one meaty hand. "It's only a question of time."

"You mean you still don't know *exactly* where they are."

"They're on the Island."

"But you don't know *where*."

"It's only a question of time!"

"It is approximately one hundred miles," Gelding said,

with no attempt to soften his tone, "from the New York City line across Long Island to Montauk Point. In spots, the Island is twenty miles wide. In land area, it is larger than Rhode Island. This is the area in which you have them *bottled up?*"

In moments of stress, the captain's left eye tended to close, and then open again, and then slowly close again, then pop open once more, and so on. It made him look as though he were winking, and in his youth he had inadvertently picked up more than one young lady that way; in fact, it still did pretty well for him.

But there were no young ladies here now. "The point," the captain told the banker, "is that they can't get *off* the Island. It's a big place, but sooner or later we'll cover it."

"What are you doing so far?"

"Until morning," the captain said, "the only thing we can do is patrol the streets, hope to find them before they get the thing under cover."

"It is almost three in the morning, well over an hour since the bank was stolen. Surely they're under cover by now."

"Maybe. At first light, we spread out more. Before we're done, we'll look inside every old barn, every abandoned factory, every empty building of any kind on the whole Island. We'll check all dead-end roads, we'll look into every bit of woods."

"You're talking, Captain, about an operation that will take a month."

"No, Mr. Gelding, I'm not. By morning, we'll have the assistance of Boy Scout troops, volunteer fire departments and other local organizations all over the Island to help in the search. We'll use the same groups and the same techniques as when we're looking for a lost child."

"The bank," Gelding said frostily, "is somewhat larger than a lost child."

"That can only help," Captain Deemer said. "We'll also have assistance from the Civil Air Patrol in scanning from the skies."

"Scanning from the skies?" The phrase seemed to take Gelding aback.

"I say we have them bottled up," Captain Deemer said, his voice rising and his left eyelid lowering, "and I say it's only a question of time till we *tighten the net!*" And he did that chicken-killing gesture again, making Lieutenant Hepplewhite in his unobserved corner wince once more.

"All right," Gelding said grudgingly. "Under the circumstances, I must admit you seem to be doing everything possible."

"Everything," agreed the captain and turned his attention to Gary Wallah, the young man from the mobile-home company. The strain of having to deal as allies with somebody who looked like Gary Wallah caused the captain's head to lower into his neck again and his left eyelid to flutter like an awning in an on-shore breeze. "Tell me about this trailer," he said, and despite his best intentions the sentence came growling out as though instead he'd said, "Up against the wall, kid." (He didn't use bad language in uniform.)

"It's a mobile home," Wallah said. "It isn't a trailer. A trailer is a little thing with wheels that you rent from U-Haul when you want to move a refrigerator. What we're talking about is a mobile home."

"I don't care if you call it a Boeing 747, boy," said the captain, no longer even caring about the growl in his voice, "just so you describe it to me."

Wallah didn't say anything for a few seconds, just glanced around the room with a little smile on his face. Finally he nodded and said, "Right on. I'm here this time to cooperate, that's what I'll do."

Captain Deemer closed his mouth firmly over the several things it occurred to him to say. He reminded himself that he really didn't *want* to fight with everybody on his own team, and he waited in controlled impatience for this goddam draft-dodging useless hippie pot-smoking disrespectful radical son of a bitch bastard to say whatever it was he was going to say.

In a neutral tone, Wallah said, "What Roamerica leased to the bank was a modified version of our Remuda model. It's fifty feet long and twelve feet wide and is usually made up as a two- or three-bedroom home in a variety of styles, but mostly either Colonial or Western. But in this case it was turned over to the bank with no interior partitions and without the usual kitchen appliances. The normal bathroom was put in; that is, the fixtures only, no walls or decor. The modifications done at the factory consisted mostly of installing a full burglar alarm system in the walls, floor and roof of the unit and strengthening the floor at the rear portion. This what you want, Cap?"

Instead of answering directly, Captain Deemer looked over at Lieutenant Hepplewhite to see if he was taking all this down the way he was supposed to; he was taking it down, but not the way he was supposed to. That is, instead of sitting at the desk like a normal human being he was standing beside it, bent over, pencil flying across paper. "Goddamit, Lieutenant," the captain shouted, "sit down before you get a humpback!"

"Yes, sir." The lieutenant zipped into the chair, then looked attentively toward Wallah.

The captain said, "You got all that so far?"

"Yes, sir."

"Good. Go ahead, buh—"

Wallah raised an eyebrow and one side of his mustache. "Hello?"

"Nothing," the captain said grumpily. "Go ahead."

"Not much more to tell. It has the usual wiring in it, to be attached to regular commercial power company lines. It has baseboard electric heating. The bathroom fixtures feed out through the bottom of the unit and are adaptable to local plumbing codes. Roamerica delivered the unit to the site connected up all power lines, water lines, sewage lines, burglar alarm lines, removed the wheels, leveled the—"

"Removed the wheels?" The captain's left eye was completely shut now, maybe for good.

"Sure," Wallah said. "It's standard procedure if you're going to—"

"Are you telling me that goddam trailer didn't have any *wheels?*"

"Mobile home. And natu—"

"Trailer!" the captain yelled. "Trailer, trailer goddam

trailer! And if it didn't have any goddam *wheels,* how did they get it away from there?"

Nobody answered. The captain stood panting in the middle of the room, head bulked down between his shoulders, like the bull after the matador's assistants have finished with him. His left eye was still closed, perhaps permanently, and his right eyelid was beginning to flutter.

Lieutenant Hepplewhite cleared his throat. Everybody jumped, as though a hand grenade had gone off, and they all stared at him. In a small voice he said, "Helicopter?"

They continued to look at him. Several slow seconds went by, and then the captain said, "Repeat that, Hepplewhite."

"Helicopter, sir," Lieutenant Hepplewhite said in the same small voice. And then, hesitant but hurrying, added, "I just thought maybe they had a helicopter and they might have come down and put ropes around it and—"

The captain glowered with his one good eye. "And take it off the Island," he finished.

"Too heavy," Wallah said. He opened his gray cloth plumber's bag and took out a toy mobile home. "Here's a scale model of the Remuda model," he said. "Remember now, it's fifty feet long. This one is pink and white; the stolen one is blue and white."

"I see the color," the captain growled. "You're sure it's too heavy?"

"No question."

"I've got a question," the captain said. Somehow he seemed to be holding the toy. Shifting it back and forth from hand to hand in some irritation, he said to Lieutenant Hepplewhite, "Phone the Army base. Find out if a helicopter could do the job."

"Yes, sir."

"And get in touch with some of the men on the scene. Have them wake neighbors, find out if anybody heard a helicopter around there tonight."

"Definitely too heavy," Wallah said. "And too long and awkward. They just couldn't do it."

"We'll find out," the captain said. "Here, take this damn thing."

Wallah took back the toy. "I thought you'd be interested," he said.

"It's the real one I'm interested in."

"Exactly," said the banker, Gelding.

Lieutenant Hepplewhite was murmuring on the phone. The captain said, "Now, if they *didn't* take it by helicopter, the question is how did they take it? What about these wheels you took off, where would they be now?"

"Stored in our assembly plant in Brooklyn," Wallah said.

"You're sure they're still there?"

"Nope."

The captain gave him the full voltage of his one good eye.

"You're *not* sure they're still there?"

"I haven't checked. But those aren't the only wheels in the world; they could have gotten wheels anywhere."

Lieutenant Hepplewhite said, "Excuse me, Mr. Wallah."

Wallah looked at him in amused surprise—probably at being called mister.

"The Army sergeant would like to talk to you."

"Sure," said Wallah. He took the phone from Hepplewhite, and they all watched him lift it to his face and say, "What's happening, man?"

The captain turned resolutely away from the conversation, and while the lieutenant answered the other phone, which had suddenly started to ring, he said to Gelding, "Don't you worry. It doesn't matter how they did it, we'll catch up with them. You can't steal a whole bank and expect to get away with it."

"I certainly hope not."

"Sir?"

The captain turned a mistrustful eye on the lieutenant. "What now?"

"Sir, the bank had been resting on a foundation of concrete blocks. The officers on the scene have found tub caulking on top of the blocks."

"Tub caulking on top of the blocks."

"Yes, sir."

"And they decided to report that."

The lieutenant blinked. He was still holding the phone. Next to him, Gary Wallah was in conversation on the other phone with the Army sergeant. "Yes, sir," the lieutenant said.

The captain nodded. He took a deep breath. "Tell them thank you," he said in a soft voice and turned to Albert Docent, the safe-company man, who hadn't as yet contributed anything. "Well, what good news do *you* have for me?" he said.

"They'll have a hell of a time with that safe," Docent said. Above the bow tie, his expression was clean-cut, dutiful and intelligent.

The captain's left eye fluttered slightly, as though it might open. He nearly smiled. *"Will* they?" he said.

Gary Wallah said, "The sergeant wants to talk to one of you people." He was offering the phone indiscriminately to both Captain Deemer and Lieutenant Hepplewhite.

"You take it, Lieutenant."

"Yes, sir."

Once again, they all watched and listened as Hepplewhite spoke with the sergeant. His part of the conversation was mostly "Uh huh" and "Is that right?" but his audience kept watching and listening anyway. Finally he finished and hung up and said, "It couldn't be done by helicopter."

The captain said, "They're sure? Positive?"

"Yes, sir."

"Good," said the captain. "Then they're still on the Island, just like I said." He turned back to Docent, the safe man. "You were saying?"

"I was saying," Docent said, "that they'll find that safe a tough nut to crack. It's one of the most modern safes we make, with the latest advances in heat-resistant and shock-resistant metals. These are advances that come from research connected with the Vietnam war. It's one of the ironic benefits of that unhappy—"

"Oh, wow," said Gary Wallah.

Docent turned to him, firm but fair. "All I'm saying," he said, "is that research has been stimulated into some—"

"Oh, wow. I mean, wow."

"I've heard all your arguments, and I can't say I entirely disagree with—"

"Wow, man."

"At this time," George Gelding said, standing at attention and looking very red-faced, "when some person or persons unknown have stolen a branch of the Capitalists' and Immigrants' Trust, and our brave boys are dying on far-flung battlefields to protect the rights of likes of you who—"

"Oh, wow."

"Now, there's much to be said on both sides, but the point is—"

"I see those flaaaaag-draped coffins, I hear the loved ones in their cottages and on the farms of America—"

"Like, really, wow."

Captain Deemer glowered at them all through the remaining slit of his right eye. A bellowed *shut up* might attract their attention—all three were talking at the same time now—but did he want them to shut up? If they stopped arguing with one another, they'd just start talking to the captain again, and he wasn't sure he wanted that.

In the middle of the melee the phone rang. Captain Deemer was aware of Lieutenant Hepplewhite answering it, but that didn't have much interest for him, either. More tub caulking, he supposed, this time in the ears of his officers.

But then Hepplewhite shouted, "Somebody saw it!" and the argument stopped as though somebody had switched off a radio. Everybody—even the captain—stared at Hepplewhite, sitting there at the desk with the phone in his hand, grinning at them with happy excitement.

Gelding said, "Well? Well?"

"A bartender," Hepplewhite said, "closing up for the night. He saw it go by, about quarter to two. Said it was going like hell. Said there was a cab off a big tractor-trailer rig pulling it."

"Quarter to two?" the captain said. "Why the hell didn't he report it till now?"

"Didn't think anything of it. He lives in Queens, and

they stopped him at a roadblock going through. That's when he found out what happened and told them he'd seen it."

"Where was this?"

"On Union Turnpike. They've got a roadblock set up there, and—"

"No," Captain Deemer said. Patiently he said, "Where did he see the bank?"

"Oh. Up by Cold Spring."

"Cold Spring. Cold Spring." The captain hurried to the map, looked at it, found Cold Spring. "Right on the county line," he said. "They're not trying to get off the Island at all. Heading the other way, up toward Huntington." He spun around. "Get that out to all units right away, Lieutenant. Last seen at one forty-five in the vicinity of Cold Spring."

"Yes, sir." Hepplewhite spoke briefly into the phone, broke the connection, dialed the dispatcher's room.

Gelding said, "You seem pleased, Captain. This is a good sign, eh?"

"The best so far. Now if we can only get to them before they open the safe and abandon the bank—"

"I don't think you have to worry too much about that, Captain," Albert Docent said. In the heat of the argument his bow tie had become twisted, but now he was calm again, and straightening it.

Captain Deemer looked at him. "Why not?"

"I was telling you about the advances that have been made in safe construction," Docent said. He glanced at Wallah, who said nothing, and looked at the captain again to say, "Given any force that will open that safe without destroying the contents, whether nitroglycerine, acid, laser, diamond-tip drill, any of the safe cracker's arsenal of equipment, it will take those thieves a minimum of twenty-four hours to break it open."

Captain Deemer broke into a broad smile.

"Captain," said the lieutenant. He was excited again.

Captain Deemer turned the broad smile on him. "Yes, Hepplewhite?"

"They found the seven guards."

"Did they! Where?"

"Asleep on Woodbury Road."

The captain was already turning toward his map, but he stopped and frowned at the lieutenant. "Asleep?"

"Yes, sir. On Woodbury Road. In a ditch beside the road."

Captain Deemer looked at Albert Docent. "We're going to *need* twenty-four hours," he said.

23

"OH, I can *do* it," Herman said. "That isn't the question."

"Tell me the question," Dortmunder said, "because I'm dying to ask it."

They had come to rest now. Murch had delivered them to an open slot in the rear of the Wanderlust Trailer Park, a kind of nomadic village far out on Long Island. The owners of the Wanderlust lived elsewhere, in a proper house, and so wouldn't be aware of the freeloader until tomorrow morning; as for the occupants of the other mobile homes here, some of them might have been awakened by the sound of the truck engine going past their units, but it isn't unheard of for people to arrive or leave a trailer park in the middle of the night.

Murch had now departed with the truck cab, which he would ditch about fifteen miles from here, at the spot where they'd already stashed the Ford station wagon that would be their getaway car. May and Murch's Mom had finished giving the place a gloss of hominess, and the idea now was that Herman would have been working on the safe since they'd left the football stadium and would have it open by the time Murch got back with the Ford. Only now Herman was saying he wouldn't.

"The question," Herman explained, "is time. This is a newer safe than I've seen before. The metal is different, the lock is different, the door is different, everything is different."

"It'll take longer," Dortmunder suggested.

"Yes."

"We can wait," Dortmunder said and looked at his watch. "It isn't even three o'clock yet. Even if we're out of here by six, six-thirty, we're still all right."

Herman shook his head.

Dortmunder turned and looked at May. They were still moving around by the light of flashlights, and it was hard to read May's expression, but it wasn't hard at all to read Dortmunder's. "I been kept out of mischief," Dortmunder said. "That's one thing for sure."

"Herman," May said, coming forward, the cigarette bobbing in the corner of her mouth, "Herman, tell us. How bad is it?"

"Lousy," Herman said.

"How lousy?"

"Terrible lousy. Rotten lousy."

"How long would it take to open the safe?"

"All day," Herman said.

"That's wonderful," said Dortmunder.

Herman looked at him. "I'm as happy about this as you are. I take pride in my work."

"I'm sure you do, Herman," May said. "But the point is, sooner or later you *could* open it."

"Given time. The original idea was I'd have all the time I wanted."

Dortmunder said, "We couldn't find a place to put this goddam thing under cover. All we could do was this—paint, curtains on the windows, put it in a trailer camp. They'll find the thing this morning, but we should have it camouflaged enough so we're clear and home and dry before they do. If we leave no later than six, six-thirty."

"Then we leave without the cash," Herman said.

May turned to Dortmunder. "Why do we have to leave?"

"Because they'll *find* this thing."

Murch's Mom came forward, carrying the flashlights. "Why will they?" she wanted to know. "It's like *The Purloined Letter,* we've got a trailer hidden in a trailer camp. We've changed the color, we put license plates on, we put curtains on the windows. How are they gonna find us?"

"Sometime in the morning," Dortmunder said, "the owner or the manager of this place will come along, and he'll know this trailer doesn't belong here. So he'll come knock on the door. And then he'll look inside." Dortmunder waved an arm to indicate what that owner or manager would see.

Murch's Mom already knew what the interior looked like, but she obediently flashed her light around anyway and said, "Mmmmm." Not very encouraging. Mobile homes come in a lot of different styles, colonial and French Provincial and Spanish and Victorian, but no one so far has decided to live in a trailer done up as Suburban Bank.

May squinted past cigarette smoke and said, "What if we pay rent on it?"

They all looked at her. Dortmunder said, "I missed a couple words there, I think."

"No, listen," she said. "This slot is empty anyway. You look out that door, you'll see maybe five other empty slots. So why don't we just stick with the trailer, and when the owner comes around in the morning we pay him his fees? Pay him his rent for a couple days, a week, whatever he wants."

Herman said, "That's not bad."

"Sure," Murch's Mom said. "Then it really is *The Purloined Letter*. They'll be looking for us, and looking for the trailer, and we'll be in the trailer in a trailer camp."

"I don't know about puh-purlayed letters, whatever it is," Dortmunder said. "But I do know about robbery. You don't . . . when you knock over a bank, you don't live in it after you knocked it over, you go away someplace else. I mean . . . that's just the way it's *done*."

Herman said, "But wait a minute, Dortmunder. We haven't knocked it over yet. That goddam safe is giving me trouble. And if we stay here, we can hook into the electricity supply, I can use decent tools, I can really do a job on that mother—uh, on that safe."

Dortmunder frowned, looking around the interior of the bank. "It makes me nervous to stay here," he said. "That's all I can tell you, maybe it means I'm old-fashioned, but it makes me nervous."

May said, "It isn't like you to give up. It just isn't your style."

Dortmunder scratched his head and looked around some more. "I know," he said. "But this is not a traditional robbery. You go in, you get what you came for, you go away. You don't set up housekeeping."

"Just for one day," Herman said. "Just till I get into that safe."

Dortmunder kept scratching, then suddenly stopped and said, "What about connecting up? The electricity and the plumbing. When they do it, what if they have to come inside?"

"We don't need the plumbing," Murch's Mom said.

"After a while we will."

May said, "They have to connect it up; it's the sanitary laws."

"There you are," Dortmunder said.

Herman said, "We'll do it ourselves."

Dortmunder looked at him with true annoyance. Every time he'd safely relegated the idea to the Impossible shelf, somebody had to come along with another suggestion. He said, "What do you mean, do it ourselves?"

"Connect everything up," Herman said. "You and me and Murch, we can do it ourselves right now. Then it's all done, and when the manager comes around in the morning Mrs. Murch goes out, or May goes out, somebody, and we pay him off. And if he wants to know how come everything's already connected up, we tell him we got in late at night, we didn't want to disturb anybody, so we did it ourselves."

May said, "You know, if we took this counter apart,

and put this piece on top of that piece, and ran it across here, then you could open this door and somebody outside wouldn't see anything strange at all. Just like a corridor in the trailer."

Murch's Mom said, "Down here, we could move this stuff out of the way, and take that chair and that chair and that table, and put them around this way like this, and then somebody could stand outside this door, too, and what would it be?"

"A disaster," Dortmunder said.

"A breakfast nook," Murch's Mom said firmly.

"They can't search every trailer on Long Island," Herman said. "They may come around to the trailer parks, the cops—"

"You just know they will," Dortmunder said.

"But they won't be looking for a green trailer with Michigan license plates and curtains in the windows and a couple nice middle-aged ladies that answer the door."

"And what if they say they want to come in?"

"Now now, Officer," May said, "my sister's just come out of the shower."

"Who is it, Myrtle?" Murch's Mom called in a high falsetto.

"Just some police officers," May called back, "wanting to know if we saw a bank go past here last night."

Dortmunder said, "You two ladies could get accessory. You could wind up working in a state-pen laundry."

"Federal pen," Murch's Mom said. "Bank robbery is a Federal rap."

"We're not worried," May said. "We've got everything figured."

"I can't tell you," Dortmunder said, "how many guys I met behind bars that said the exact same thing."

Herman said, "Well, I'm going to stay, that's all. That goddam safe is a challenge to me."

"We're all going to stay," May said. She looked at Dortmunder. "Aren't we?"

Dortmunder sighed.

"Somebody coming," Herman said.

Murch's Mom doused the flashlights, and the only illumination was the red glow of May's cigarette. They heard the car approach, they saw its headlights flash by the windows. The engine stopped, the door opened and closed, and a few seconds later the bank door opened and Murch stuck his head in. "Set?" he called.

Dortmunder sighed again as Murch's Mom switched the flashlights back on. "Come on in here, Stan," Dortmunder said. "Let's talk."

24

VICTOR said:

"Steely-eyed Dortmunder surveyed his work. The wheels were under the very floor of the bank itself. Hungry, desperate men, their hat brims pulled low, his gang had worked with him beneath the shield of night to install those wheels, turning the innocent-appearing bank into an . . .

ENGINE OF GREED!

"I myself had been one of those men, as recounted in the earlier tale, *Wheels of Terror!,* in this same series. And now, the final moment had come, the moment that had filled our every waking thought for all these days and weeks of preparation.

" 'This is the payoff,' Dortmunder snarled softly. 'Tonight we get the whole swag.'

" 'Right, boss,' whispered Kelp eagerly, his scarred face twisting into a brutal smile.

"I repressed a shudder at that smile. If my companions but knew the truth about me, how that smile would alter its effect! I wouldn't last long with this crew of desperate ruffians, if ever they penetrated my disguise. I was known to them as Lefty the Lip McGonigle, late of Sing Sing, a tough customer and no friend of the law. I had used the McGonigle monicker twice before, once to capture the evil *Specter of the Drive-In!* and once to invade the criminal-infested precincts of the dread Sing Sing itself, that time to solve the slaying of the stoolie Sad Sam Sassanack, in the adventure later related under the title *Brutes Behind Bars!*

"And now, I was Lefty the Lip yet again, in the course of my duty to my God and my Nation as . .

SECRET AGENT J-27!

"None of Dortmunder's hoods had ever seen my real face. None knew my real name. None knew the—"

"Victor?"

Victor leaped, dropping the microphone. Spinning around in his chair, he saw Stan Murch standing in the open bookcase, framed by the night behind him. Victor was so deeply into his story line by this time that he recoiled when he realized he was looking at one of Dortmunder's men.

Murch took a step forward, his expression concerned. "Something the matter, Victor?"

"No no," Victor said shakily, shaking his head. "You just—you just startled me," he added lamely.

"Kelp told me this was where I'd probably find you," Murch said. "That's why I'm here."

"Yes, of course," Victor said inanely. Looking down, he saw that the cassette was still running and switched it off. "This is where I am," he said aimlessly.

"There's been a problem at the bank," Murch said. "We all got to assemble again."

"Where?" Victor asked interrogatively.

"At the bank."

"Yes, but where's the bank?" Victor pursued puzzledly. He had last seen the bank in the high-school football field and didn't know precisely where it would be kept for the rest of the night.

"You can follow me in your car," Murch said. "You ready?"

"I suppose so," Victor said uncertainly, looking around the garage. "But what's gone wrong?" he asked belatedly.

"Herman says it's a new kind of safe, it'll take him all day to break into it."

"All day!" Victor exploded, aghast. "But surely the police—"

"We're setting it up with a front," Murch said. And then added, "We're in kind of a press for time, Victor, so if you could—"

"Oh, of course!" Victor said abashedly. He leaped to his feet, then picked up the cassette and microphone and stuffed them in his jacket pocket. "Ready," he announced earnestly.

They left, Victor carefully switching off the lights and locking the door behind himself, and the two of them walked down the dark driveway to the street. While Murch got into the station wagon parked there, Victor hurried across the street to the garage he rented from a neighbor, in which he kept his Packard. This was a more modern garage than his own, with an electronically operated lift door that he could raise or lower by touching a button on the dashboard of the car. For several months he'd been trying to get up enough nerve to ask his neighbor's permission to do some work on the outside of the building, but so far hadn't developed sufficient courage. What he wanted to do was make the front look like a seemingly abandoned warehouse, without doors, so that a section of wall would appear to lift when the dashboard button was pushed. There were two difficulties with this conception. First, he didn't know what cover story to give the owner for wanting to make the change, and, second, a seemingly abandoned warehouse would look definitely out of place in this neighborhood—particularly in somebody's back yard. Still, it was a pleasant idea, and he might yet be able to work something out.

At night, though, the effect was almost as good with the building just the way it was. Victor entered through the side door of the garage, switched on the dim red bulb he'd installed in the overhead light fixture, and by its darkroom-like illumination removed the plastic cover from the Packard, folding it like a flag and then putting it away on its shelf. Next he got into the car, took the cassette and microphone from his pocket and put them on the seat beside him, and started the engine. The Packard motor grumbled quietly but menacingly in the enclosed space. Smiling to himself, Victor turned on the parking lights only and pushed the button that caused the door to slide up. With a distinct sense of drama, he tapped the accelerator and steered the Packard out into the night, then pushed the button again and watched in the rear-view mirror as the door folded down once more behind him, the red-lit view of the garage interior narrowing from the top and at last disappearing completely. Only then did he switch on his headlights.

Murch seemed impatient. He was revving the engine of the stolen station wagon, and the instant Victor and the Packard reached the street he shot away from the curb and dashed away down the street. Victor followed at a more stately pace, but soon had to pick it up a little if he was going to keep Stan in sight at all.

The first time they were stopped at a red light, Victor ran the tape back a bit in the cassette, found the spot where he'd left off, and took it from there, dictating into the microphone as he followed Murch and his scuttling station wagon across Long Island:

"None of Dortmunder's hoods had ever seen my real face. None knew my real name. None knew the truth about me, and it would be curtains for me if they did!

"Now, gimlet-eyed Dortmunder nodded in satisfaction. 'Forty-eight hours from now,' he boasted evilly, 'that proud bank will be ours! Nothing can stop us now!' "

25

"IF YOU'LL put the *flashlight* on my *work*," Herman said, "things'll go a lot faster."

"Sure," Kelp said. He adjusted the beam. "I was shielding it with my body," he said.

"Well, don't shield it from *me*."

"Okay," Kelp said.

"And don't breathe down the back of my neck like that."

"Right," Kelp said. He moved half an inch.

Suddenly into Herman's head came the replay of a television commercial from a few years back: *Sure, you're irritable. Who wouldn't be? But don't take it out on him. Take . . .* Take what? What was the product? Sounds like it should have been pot, but it probably wasn't.

The distraction of that chain of thought was a pleasant interlude, three or four seconds long, which calmed him perhaps as much as the forgotten product would have done. Herman took a deep, slow breath, to calm himself even more, and returned his attention to the task at hand.

He was squatting right now like a Masai warrior in front of a black metal box emerging from the ground directly in front of the hitch end of the bank. Power and water and sewer lines terminated in this box, and it was Herman's simple job at the moment to remove the padlock from the lid and open the box. And it was taking too long.

"Normally," Herman said, speaking more gently than before, but still with a rasp of irritation he couldn't quite get rid of, "I'm very good at locks."

"Sure," Kelp said. "Naturally."

The padlock clicked and jittered in Herman's long, thin fingers. "It's just that safe," he said. "It's shaken my self-confidence."

"You're still the best," Kelp said. Not in a boosting way, but conversationally, as though commenting on the weather.

The padlock skittered away from Herman's fingers and tick-ticked against the metal lid. "I'm also very good at self-analysis," he said. His voice quivered again with barely controlled rage. "I figure out just where I'm at. And"—his voice rising, speeding up—"it doesn't *do a goddam bit of good!*"

"You'll be fine," Kelp said. He patted Herman on the shoulder.

Herman flinched away from the touch like a horse. "I am going to get this thing," he said grimly and sat down on the ground in front of the box. Legs folded tailor-fashion, he leaned over the box till his nose was almost touching the lock.

"I'm having a little trouble," Kelp said, "keeping the light on the work."

"Shut up," Herman said.

Kelp knelt beside him and beamed the light principally at Herman's right eye, which was glaring at the lock.

The problem was, they didn't want to break it. In the morning, they would tell the trailer-court owner or manager that they'd found the thing unlocked and just hooked everything up themselves. If he saw his padlock in normal condition, he probably wouldn't raise a fuss. But if he found it broken, he might not believe the story, and then he might make trouble.

That was the problem about why the padlock had to be picked rather than plucked. The deeper problem, Herman's continuing inability to pick it, was very simply caused by that son-of-a-bitch safe. Half a dozen small tools from his black bag were already spread across the box lid, and he was poking away at the padlock's keyhole with yet another small tool right now—the other end of which was currently endangering his eye—and he just couldn't keep his mind on what he was doing. He'd slip the tool into the padlock and his eyes would glaze as his mind drifted back to consider once again the safe inside the bank. He had no saw or drill—including the diamond tip—that would get through that metal. He had stripped away the combination plate and mechanism, but it had led nowhere. He had tried peeling the door and had bent his favorite medium-length bar. An explosion strong enough to rip open the safe would also destroy everything inside it and would probably open the trailer up like an avocado at the same time.

What it came down to was the circular hole. For the circular hole, you attached a suction clamp to the side of the safe, with a central rod extending straight out. An L-shaped arm swung from the rod, with a handle at the elbow and a clamp at the wrist for drill bits. A bit was put in place, so that it scraped against the side of the safe, and then the handle was turned in a large circle, over and over and over again. As each bit was worn away, a new one was added. It was the slowest and most primitive kind of safe-cracking, but it was the only thing that could possibly work against that goddam bastard son of a bitch—

The padlock. His mind had drifted again, and he'd just been sitting there on the ground, poking aimlessly into the keyhole with the small tool. "God *damn* it," he muttered, and clenched his teeth, and gripped the padlock so hard his fingers ached.

The thing was, sometimes you had to go back to basics. Herman knew the most sophisticated ways to get into safes and vaults and had used them all at one time or another. The ELD, for instance, Electronic Listening Device; attach it to the front of the safe, put the earphones on and listen to the tumblers while you turn the combination. Or ways of putting just a little plastic explosive in two places at the edge of the door, where the hinges are on the inside, and then going next door and setting them off by radio signal and coming back to find the door lying on its face on the floor and not a sheet of paper wrinkled inside. Or—

The padlock. He'd done it again.

"Rrrrrrr," Herman said.

"Here comes somebody."

"That was me growling."

"No. Headlights." Kelp switched off the flashlight.

Herman looked around and saw the headlights turning in from the highway. "It can't be Murch already," he said.

"Well," Kelp said doubtfully, "it *is* almost four o'clock."

Herman stared at him. "Four o'clock? I've been at this, I've been here for . . . ? Give me that light!"

"Well, we're not sure it's them yet." The headlights were slowly approaching past the darkened trailers.

"I don't *need* the goddam light," Herman said, and while the headlights came up close enough to show the car behind them, and the car parked, and Murch got out, Herman picked the padlock by feel alone, and when Kelp next turned the flashlight on, Herman was putting his tools away. "It's done," he said.

"You got it!"

"Of course I got it." Herman glared at him. "What do you sound so surprised for?"

"Well, I just . . . Uh, here's Stan and Victor."

But it was just Murch. He strolled over and gestured at the black box and said, "You get it open?"

"Listen," Herman said angrily, "just because I'm having trouble with that safe . . ."

Murch looked startled. "I just wanted to know," he said.

Kelp said, "Where's Victor?"

"Here he comes now," Murch said and gestured with his thumb toward the court entrance as another pair of headlights made the turn. "He really hangs well back," Murch said. "I was surprised. I almost lost him a couple times."

Dortmunder had come out of the bank and now walked over to say, "There's a hell of a lot of talk out here. Let's keep it down."

"The padlock's open," Herman told him.

Dortmunder glanced at him and then looked at his watch. "That's good," he said. There was no expression in either his face or his voice.

"Look," Herman said aggressively, but then didn't have anything else to say and just stood there.

Victor came over, walking slightly lopsided and looking stunned. "Boy," he said.

Dortmunder said, "Let's go inside where we can talk. You boys be able to fix things up out here?"

Kelp and Murch would be doing the tie-in of power and water and sewer lines. Kelp said, "Sure, we'll work it out."

"You've got some bent pipes there," Dortmunder said, "where we ripped them when we took the bank."

"No problem," Murch said. "I brought some pipe in the car. We'll rig something up."

"But quiet," Dortmunder said.

"Sure," Murch said.

The efficiency all around him was making Herman nervous. "I'm going in and work on that safe," he said.

Dortmunder and Victor came along with him, and Dortmunder said to Victor, "Did Stan tell you the situation?"

"Sure. Herman's having trouble getting the safe open, so we're going to stay here for a while."

Herman hunched his shoulders and glowered straight ahead, but said nothing.

As they were climbing up into the bank, Victor said, "That Stan really drives, doesn't he?"

"That's his job," Dortmunder said, and Herman winced at that one, too.

"Boy," Victor said. "You try to keep up with him . . . boy."

Inside the trailer, May and Murch's Mom had set up a couple of flashlights on pieces of furniture so there was some light to work by and were now cleaning the place up a little. "I think we've got a full deck of cards here," Murch's Mom told Dortmunder. "I just found the three of clubs over by the safe."

"That's fine," Dortmunder said. He turned to Herman. "You want any help?"

"No!" Herman snapped, but a second later said, "I mean yes. Sure, of course."

"Victor, you go with Herman."

"Sure."

May said to Dortmunder, "We need you to move some furniture."

While Dortmunder went off to join the spring-cleaning brigade, Herman said to Victor, "I've made a decision."

Victor looked alert.

"I am going," Herman said, "to attack that safe by every method known to man. All at once."

"Sure," Victor said. "What should I do?"

"You," Herman told him, "will turn the handle."

26

"FRANKLY," May said, the cigarette bobbing in the corner of her mouth, "I could make better coffee than this if I started with dirt." She dropped a seven of hearts on the eight of diamonds Dortmunder had led.

"I took what they had," Murch said. "It was the only place I could find open." He carefully slid a five of diamonds under the seven of diamonds.

"I'm not blaming you," May said. "I'm just commenting."

Murch's Mom put down her own coffee container, frowned at her hand and at last gave an elaborate sigh and said, "Oh, well." She played the jack of diamonds and drew in the trick.

"Look out," Murch said. "Mom's shooting the moon."

His mother gave him a dirty look. "Mom's shooting the

moon, Mom's shooting the moon. You know so much. I *had* to take that trick."

"That's okay," Murch said calmly. "I got stoppers."

May was sitting by the partially open door of the trailer, where she could look out and see the blacktop street all the way down to the court entrance. It was now ten after seven in the morning and fully light. Half a dozen seedy cars had left here in the last half hour, as residents went off to work, but no one had as yet arrived to question this new trailer's presence—neither a trailer-court manager nor the police.

While waiting, May and Murch's Mom were running a rousing game of hearts in the pseudo-breakfast nook they'd set up by the door toward the front end of the trailer, farthest from the safe. Back at the other end, hidden behind a new floor-to-ceiling partition created from sections of counter, Herman was working away steadily at the safe, assisted by the men in groups of two. Kelp and Victor were back there with him now, while Dortmunder and Murch were sitting in at the card game. At eight o'clock, the men would switch.

So far, there had been two small *crump* sounds from the other side of the counter as Herman had tried minor explosions which had failed to accomplish anything, and occasionally there was the whir of a power tool or the buzz of a saw intermixed with the steady rasp of the circular drill, but up till now very little seemed to be happening. Ten minutes ago, when Dortmunder and Murch had finished their six-to-seven shift, May had asked them how things were going. "I won't say he hasn't made a dent in it," Dortmunder had said. "He's made a dent in it." And he'd rubbed his shoulder, having spent most of the previous hour turning a handle in a large circle.

In the meantime, the bank had been made more livable and homelike. The electricity and bathroom were both working, the floor had been swept, the furniture rearranged and the curtains put up on the windows. It was only too bad the bank hadn't come equipped with a kitchen; the hamburgers and doughnuts Murch had brought back from the all-night diner were almost edible, but the coffee was probably against the anti-pollution laws.

"Anything?" Dortmunder asked.

May had been gazing toward the street, thinking about kitchens and food and coffee. She switched her attention to Dortmunder and said, "No, I was just daydreaming."

"You're tired, that's why," Murch's Mom said. "We all are, staying up all night. I'm not as young as I used to be." She played the ace of diamonds.

"Ho ho," her son said. "Not shooting the moon, huh?"

"I'm too clever for you," she told him. "While you big-mouth, I get rid of all my dangerous winners." She had taken her neck brace off, despite her son's complaints, and was now hunched over her cards like a gambling squirrel.

"Here comes somebody," May said.

Dortmunder said, "Law?"

"No. The manager, I think."

A blue-and-white station wagon had just turned in at the entrance and stopped beside the small white-clapboard office shack. A smallish man in a dark suit got out of the car, and when May saw him start to unlock the office door she put down her cards and said, "That's him. I'll be back."

Murch said, "Mom, put the brace on."

"I will not."

They still didn't have steps for the trailer. May clambered awkwardly down to the ground, flipped a cigarette ember away from the corner of her mouth and lit a new one as she walked down the row to the office.

The man at the sloppy desk inside had the thin, nervous, dehydrated look of a reformed drunk—the look of a man who at any instant may go back to sleeping in alleys while clutching a pint bottle of port. He gave May a terrified stare and said, "Yes, Miss? Yes?"

"We're moving in for a week," May said. "I wanted to pay you."

"A week? A trailer?" He seemed baffled by everything. Maybe it was just the early hour that was getting to him.

"That's right," May said. "How much is it for a week?"

"Twenty-seven fifty. Where's the, uh, where do you have your trailer?"

"Back there on the right," May said, pointing through the wall.

He frowned, bewildered. "I didn't hear you drive in."

"We came in last night."

"Last *night!*" He leaped to his feet, knocking a pile of forms slithering from the desk to the floor. While May watched him in some amazement, he raced out the front door. She shook her head and stooped to pick up the fallen papers.

He was back a minute later, saying, "You're right. I never even noticed it when I . . . Here, you don't have to do that."

"All done," May said. Straightening, she put the pile of forms back on the desk, causing some sort of seismic disturbance, because another stack of papers promptly toppled off the desk on the other side.

"Leave them, leave them," the nervous man said.

"I think I will." May moved over to let him get back to his seat behind the desk, and then she sat in the room's only other chair, facing him. "Anyway," she said, "we want to stay for a week."

"There's some forms to fill out." He started opening and slamming desk drawers, doing it far too rapidly to see anything inside them in the milliseconds when they were open. "While you're doing that," he said, opening and closing, opening and closing, "I'll go hook up the utilities."

"We already did that."

He stopped, with a drawer open, and blinked at her. "But it's locked," he said.

May took the padlock out of her sweater pocket, where it had been stretching the material even worse than her usual cigarettes. "This was on the ground beside it," she said and reached forward to put it on a pile of papers in front of him. "We thought it might be yours."

"It *wasn't* locked?" He stared at the padlock in horror, as though it were a shrunken head.

"Nope."

"If the boss . . ." He licked his lips, then stared at May in mute appeal.

"I won't tell," she promised. His nervousness was making her nervous, too, and she was in a hurry to get finished with him and out of here.

"He can be very . . ." He shook his head, then glanced down at the open drawer, seemed surprised to see it open, then frowned at it and drew out some papers. "Here they are," he said.

May spent the next ten minutes filling out forms. She wrote that the trailer had four occupants: Mrs. Hortense Davenport (herself); her sister, Mrs. Winifred Loomis (Murch's Mom); and Mrs. Loomis' two sons, Stan (Murch) and Victor (Victor). Dortmunder and Kelp and Herman did not exist on the forms May filled out.

The manager grew gradually calmer as time went by, as though slowly getting used to May's presence, and was even risking shaky little smiles when May handed over the last of the forms and the twenty-seven dollars and fifty cents. "I hope your stay at Wanderlust is just great," he said.

"Thank you, I'm sure it will be," May said, getting to her feet, and the manager suddenly looked terrified again and moved all his extremities at once, causing great land shifts of paper on his desk. May, baffled, looked over her shoulder and saw the room filling with state troopers. May stifled a nervous start of her own, but she didn't need to; the manager's contortions had riveted the troopers' attentions.

"Well, bye now," May said and walked through the troopers—there were only two of them after all—toward the door. The thump behind her was either the padlock or the manager hitting the floor; she didn't turn to see which, but kept going, and strode hurriedly up the gravel drive toward the bank. As she approached it, she saw it suddenly rock slightly on its wheels, and then settle down again. *Another of Herman's explosions,* she thought, and a few seconds later a puff of white smoke came out a vent on the trailer roof. *They've picked a Pope,* she thought.

Dortmunder was waiting in the doorway to give her a hand up. "Whoop, thanks," she said. "The cops are here."

"I saw them. We'll get back of the partition."

"Right."

Murch's Mom said, "Let's not get those cards mixed up. Everybody hold onto your own hand."

Murch said, "Mom, will you please put the brace on?"

"For the last time, no."

"You could blow the whole case for us right here."

She stared at him. "I am standing in a stolen bank," she said, "which is about nine felonies rolled into one already, and you're worried about a lawsuit with an insurance company?"

"If we get picked up on this thing," Murch said, "we'll need all the cash we can lay our hands on for the defense."

"That's a cheerful thought," May said. She was standing by the door, looking out toward the office.

Dortmunder had gone around behind the partition to join Herman and Kelp, and now all sound stopped from back there. A second later, Victor came out and said, "So they're here, are they?" He had a big smile on his face.

"Just coming out of the office," May said. She shut the door and went over to look out a window instead.

"Remember," Victor said, "they can't come in without a warrant."

"I know, I know."

But the troopers made no attempt to come in. They walked down the gravel roadway between the lines of trailers, looking this way and that, and gave the green-painted bank no more than a passing glance.

Victor was watching out another window. "It's starting to rain," he said. "They'll want to get back in the car."

It was, and they did. A slight sprinkle had developed, and the troopers walked a bit faster on their way back down the line of trailers toward their car. May, looking up, saw heavy clouds coming on fast from the west. "It's really going to come down," she said.

"What do we care?" Victor said. "We're warm and dry inside this bank here." He looked around with that big smile on his face and said, "They even have electric baseboard heat."

Murch's Mom said, "Are they gone?"

"Just getting in their car," May said. "There they go." She turned from the window, and now she too was smiling. "I suddenly realize," she said, "that I was very nervous." She took the stub of cigarette from her mouth and looked at it. "I just lit this," she said.

"Let's play cards," Murch's Mom said. "Dortmunder! Come on out and play cards."

Dortmunder came out, Victor went back in with Herman and Kelp, the four outside sat down to play cards again, and Murch's Mom shot the moon. Murch said, "See? See? I told you!"

"So you did," Murch's Mom said. She smiled at her son and riffled the cards as she shuffled.

Ten minutes later there was a knock at the door. Everybody at the table stared, and May quickly got up to look out the nearest window. "It's somebody with an umbrella," she announced. It was really pouring out there now, puddles everywhere.

"Get rid of him," Dortmunder said. "I'll go back by the safe again."

"Right."

May waited till Dortmunder was out of sight, then opened the door and looked out at the nervous manager, more nervous than ever and miserable-looking under the black umbrella. "Uh," May said. How could she avoid inviting him in, with all that rain?

He said something, but the drumming of the rain on both the bank roof and his umbrella drowned out the words. May said, "What?"

Shrilly, he yelled, "I don't want any trouble!"

"That's wonderful!" May shouted back. "Neither do I!"

"Look!"

He was pointing down. May leaned forward, getting her hair wet, and looked at the ground beside the trailer, and it was pale green. "Oh, for God's sake," she said and looked to left and right. The bank was blue and white again. "Oh, good Christ," she said.

"I don't want any trouble!" the manager shouted again.

May took her head in from the rain. "Come on in," she invited.

He took a step back, shaking his head and his free hand. "No no. No trouble."

May called to him, "What are you going to do?"

"I don't want you here!" he yelled. "The boss would kick me out! No trouble, no trouble!"

"You won't call the police?"

"Just go away! Go away and I won't call them and it never happened!"

May tried to think. "Give us an hour," she said.

"Too long!"

"We have to get a truck. We don't have a truck here."

His quandary was making him so nervous he was hopping from foot to foot, as though he had to go to the bathroom. Maybe, with all the rain beating down, he did. "All right," he yelled at last. "But no more than an hour!"

"I promise!"

"I'll have to unhook you! The water and electricity!"

"All right! All right!"

He fidgeted out there until she realized he was waiting for her to shut the door. Should she thank him? No, he didn't want thanks, he wanted reassurance. "You won't have any trouble!" she yelled at him, and waved, and shut the door.

Dortmunder was standing beside her. "I heard," he said.

"We'll have to take it somewhere else," she said.

"Or give up."

Herman and Kelp had wandered out from behind the

partition. Herman said, "Give up? I've just begun to fight!"

Kelp said, "What's the problem? How'd he tip to us?"

May told him, "We used water-base paint. The rain washed it off."

Herman said, "We can't give up, that's all. We just have to take it someplace else."

Dortmunder said, "With every cop on Long Island out looking for it. And with the green paint gone. And with no place in mind to put it."

Murch said, "And no truck to drive it anywhere."

Kelp said, "That's never a problem, Stan. Trucks are never a problem. Trust me."

Murch gave him a glum look.

Victor said, "In this rain, there won't be much of a search."

"When you're looking," Dortmunder said, "for something fifty feet long and twelve feet wide, colored blue and white, you don't *need* much of a search."

May had been silent during all this, thinking about things. She had no particular craving for money herself, and so didn't care so much about the contents of the safe as that the job be successful. Dortmunder was gloomy enough in his natural state; life with him if this robbery failed would be about as cheerful as a soap opera. "I tell you what," she said. "I got us an hour here."

The lights went off. Gray and rainy illumination seeped in through the windows, depressing everyone even further.

"An hour," Dortmunder said, "is just enough time for us all to go home and get to bed and make believe none of this ever happened."

"We have two cars," May said. "We can spend that hour looking for someplace to move. If we don't find anything, we give up."

"Fine," Herman said. "And I'll keep working on the safe." He hurried back behind the partition.

"It's getting cold in here," Murch's Mom said.

"You'd be warmer with the brace on," her son said.

She gave him a look.

Dortmunder sighed. "The thing that scares me," he said, "is that we probably *will* find a place."

27

DORTMUNDER said, "I suppose it's unfair to blame you for this job."

"That's right," Kelp said. He was driving, and Dortmunder was in the front seat beside him.

"But I do," Dortmunder said.

Kelp gave him an aggrieved look and faced front again. "That isn't fair," he said.

"Nevertheless."

They had until nine-thirty to get back to the bank, and it was now about nine-fifteen. Kelp and Dortmunder and Murch had started out in this station wagon together, until Kelp had found a truck big enough to do the job. It said HORSES on the sides, and the interior had a slight smell of stable to it, but it was empty. Kelp had started it up and turned it over to Murch, who had taken it away to the trailer court. Now, Kelp and Dortmunder were roaming the earth looking for somewhere to move the bank. Victor and Murch's Mom were doing the same thing in Victor's Packard.

"We'd better get back," Dortmunder said. "We aren't going to find anything."

"We might," Kelp said. "Why be so pessimistic?"

"Because we covered all this ground last week," Dortmunder said, "and there wasn't any place to hide the bank then. So why would there be someplace now?"

"Just five minutes more," Kelp said. "Then we'll head back."

"You can't see anything in this rain anyway," Dortmunder said.

"You never know," Kelp said. "We might get lucky."

Dortmunder looked at him, but Kelp was concentrating on his driving. Dortmunder considered several things he might say, but none of them seemed adequate, so after a while he turned his head and looked out the windshield at all the rain and listened to the wipers clicking back and forth.

"It's really coming down," Kelp said.

"I see it."

"You don't usually get a rain like this on a Friday," Kelp said.

Dortmunder looked at him again.

"No, I mean it," Kelp said. "Usually you get this kind of a rain on a Sunday."

Dortmunder said, "Are the five minutes up?"

"One minute to go. Keep looking for a place."

"Sure," Dortmunder said and looked out the windshield again.

The only good thing was the absence of cops. They'd seen a couple of patrol cars, but no more than normal; the search was obviously being hampered by the rain.

It seemed to Dortmunder, sitting there in the stolen station wagon while Kelp optimistically dragged him around through all this rain on a wild goose chase, that this was the story of his life. His luck was never all good, but it was never all bad either. It was a nice combination of the two, balanced so exactly that they canceled each other out. The same rain that washed away the green paint also loused up the police search. They stole the bank, but they couldn't get into the safe. On and on.

Dortmunder sighed and looked at his watch. "Your minute is up," he said.

Reluctantly, Kelp said, "Okay, I guess so." Then he said, "I'll take a swing around and head back that way."

"Go straight back," Dortmunder said.

"I don't want to go back the same roads. What's the point of that?"

"What's the point of the whole thing?"

"You're just depressed," Kelp said. "I'll turn right at that light up there and swing back that way."

Dortmunder was about to tell him to make a U-turn, but memories arose and he changed his mind. "Just so we're back by nine-thirty," he said, though he knew they wouldn't be.

"Oh, sure," Kelp said. "Definitely."

Dortmunder slumped in the corner and fantasized a return to the trailer in which May would meet him at the door by saying, "Herman opened it!" Then Herman would appear, smiling, holding handfuls of money. "Well, I got it," he'd say. Murch's Mom would be seen kicking her neck brace into the rain, shouting, "We don't need that lawsuit money any more!" Victor would stand in the background, smiling, as though waiting his turn to come forward and recite "The Boy Stood on the Burning Deck."

Kelp slammed on the brakes, and the station wagon skidded dangerously to the right. Dortmunder, jolted out of his daydream and practically into the glove compartment, shouted, "Hey! Hey, watch it!" He stared out front, and there was nothing in front of them; just the top of a hill they'd been driving up, a long gradual slope with nothing at the top, no reason at all for Kelp to slam his brakes on that way.

"Look at that!" Kelp shouted and pointed at nothing.

But Dortmunder looked instead out the rear window, saying, "You want another rear-end collision? That's your trademark? What the hell are you doing?"

"All right, I'll drive off the road. But will you take a look at that?"

Kelp drove the station wagon onto a gravel parking lot, and Dortmunder at last looked at what he was so excited about. "I see it," he said. "So what?"

"Don't you get it?"

"No."

Kelp pointed again. "We put the trailer right *there*," he said. "See what I mean?"

Dortmunder stared. "Well, God damn it," he said.

"It'll work," Kelp said.

Dortmunder couldn't help it; against his better judgment, he was smiling. "Son of a bitch," he said.

"That's right," said Kelp. "That's absolutely right."

28

"I HATE RAIN," Captain Deemer said.

"Yes, sir," said Lieutenant Hepplewhite.

"I always have hated rain," Captain Deemer said. "But never as much as today."

The two officers were in the back seat of the patrol car the captain was using as his mobile headquarters during the search for the elusive bank. In the front were two uniformed patrolmen, the driver on the left and a man to operate the radio on the right. The radio was the contact not only with the precinct but also with other cars and with other organizations engaged in the bank hunt. Unfortunately, what the radio was mostly contacting was static, a fuzzing and butsing and crackling that filled the car like the aural expression of the captain's nervous system.

The captain leaned forward, resting one heavy hand on the seat-back near the driver's head. "Can't you do anything with that goddam radio?"

"It's the rain, sir," the radio man said. "The weather is doing this."

"I know goddam well the goddam weather is doing it," the captain said. "I asked you can't you do anything about it."

"Well, we get pretty good reception when we're on a hill," the radio man said. "Driving along the flat, though, all I get is this static."

"I hear it," the captain said. He poked the driver on the shoulder and said, "Find me a hill."

"Yes, sir."

The captain leaned back and brooded at Lieutenant Hepplewhite. "A hill," he said, as though hills were in themselves an insult.

"Yes, sir."

"A mobile headquarters, and I can't contact anybody unless I stand still on a hilltop. You call that mobile?"

Lieutenant Hepplewhite looked tortured as he tried to figure out whether the proper response was *yes, sir* or *no, sir.*

Neither was needed. Captain Deemer faced front again and said, "You found a hill yet?"

"I believe there's one up ahead, sir," said the driver. "Hard to tell in this rain."

"I hate rain," said the captain. He glowered out at it, and no one spoke as the mobile headquarters started up the long gradient of the hill. The radio spackled and fizzed, the windshield wipers swish-clicked, the rain drummed on the car top, and the captain's right eyelid fluttered soundlessly.

"Shall I pull in by the diner, sir?"

The captain stared at the back of the driver's head and considered leaning forward and biting him through the neck. "Yes," he said.

"I guess the insurance company paid off," the radio man said.

The captain frowned. "What are you talking about?"

"The diner, sir," the radio man said. "They had a bad fire last year, burned to the ground."

"Well, it's back now," Lieutenant Hepplewhite said.

"Doesn't look open," the radio man said.

The captain wasn't feeling kindly toward irrelevancies. "We're not here to talk about the diner," he said. "We're here to contact headquarters."

"Yes, sir," everybody said.

The diner was set back from the road, fronted by a gravel parking lot, with a large sign out by the road, reading, MCKAY'S DINER. The driver parked near this sign, and the radio man went to work on contacting headquarters. After a minute, the static receded and a tinny voice was heard, as though they'd reached somebody who lived in an empty dog-food can. "I've got headquarters," the radio man said.

"Good," said the captain. "Tell them where we are. Where the hell are we?"

"McKay's Diner, sir."

The captain lowered his head, as though he might charge. "When I say where are we," he said, "I do not want an answer I can read off a sign right outside the goddam window. When I say where are we, I want to know—"

"Near Sagaponack, sir," the radio man said.

"Near Sagaponack."

"Yes, sir."

"Tell headquarters that."

"Yes, sir."

"Find out what's going on, if anything."

"Yes, sir."

"Tell them we'll be here until further notice."

"Yes, sir."

"Until the bank is found, or the rain stops, or I go berserk."

The radio man blinked. "Yes, sir," he said.

"Whichever comes first."

"Yes, sir."

The captain turned to Lieutenant Hepplewhite, who was looking very pale. "Even as a child I hated rain," the captain said. "I used to have a Popeye doll that you could punch and it would fall over and come back up again. It was as tall as I was, with a weighted bottom. Rainy days, I used to take that Popeye doll down in the basement and kick the shit out of it."

"Yes, sir," said the lieutenant.

The captain's eyelid drooped. "I'm getting tired of hearing 'Yes, sir' all the time," he said.

"Yes, sir," said the liutenant.

The radio man said, "Sir?"

The captain turned his heavy head.

"Sir," the radio man said, "I told headquarters our position, and they said there's nothing to report."

"Of course," said the captain.

"They say the search is being hampered by the rain."

The captain squinted. "They took the trouble to point that out, did they?"

"Yes, sir."

"Uh," said Lieutenant Hepplewhite warningly.

The captain looked at him. "Lieutenant?"

"Nothing, sir."

"What time is it, Lieutenant?"

"Ten-fifteen, sir."

"I'm hungry." The captain looked past the lieutenant at the diner. "Why don't you go get us coffee and Danish, Lieutenant? My treat."

"There's a sign in the window says they're closed, sir."

The radio man said, "Probably not ready to open yet after the fire. Their other place got burned right to the ground."

"Lieutenant," said the captain, "go over there and knock on the door and see if there's anybody in there. If there is, ask them if they can open up just enough to give us coffee and Danish."

"Yes, sir," said the lieutenant. Then, hurriedly: "I mean, uh—"

"And if not coffee and Danish," said the captain, "then whatever they can do for us we'll appreciate. Will you tell them that, Lieutenant?"

"Uh . . . I will, sir."

"Thank you," said the captain and leaned back in the corner to brood out the window at the rain.

The lieutenant got out of the car and was immediately drenched right through his uniform raincoat. It was really pouring, really and truly coming down like nobody's business. Lieutenant Hepplewhite slogged through puddles toward the diner, noting just how closed it looked. Besides the hand-lettered CLOSED sign in one window, there was the absence of any lights in there.

The whole structure had an aura about it of being not yet ready to do business. Charred and blackened remnants of the previous diner were all around the new one, not yet cleared away. The new one was still on its wheels, with no skirting of any kind; looking through the underneath space, Lieutenant Hepplewhite could see the wheels of a car and a truck parked behind the diner, the only indication that there might be somebody around here after all.

What struck the lieutenant most about this diner was an atmosphere of failure all around it. It was the kind of small business you looked at, and you knew at once they'd go bankrupt within six months. Partly, of course, it was the rain and the general gloom of the day that did that, and partly it was the new diner sitting on the ashes of the old; but it was also the windows. They were too small. People like a diner with big windows, the lieutenant thought, so they can look out and watch the traffic.

There were two doors in the front of the diner, but no steps up to either one. The lieutenant splashed along to the nearest and knocked on it and anticipated no answer at all. In fact, he was just about to turn away when the door did open slightly and a thin middle-aged woman stood looking out and down at him. She had a cigarette in the corner of her mouth, which waggled as she said, "What do you want?"

"We were wondering," the lieutenant said, "if we could get some coffee and Danish." He had to put his head back and look up when talking to her, which was uncomfortable under the circumstances. The bill of his cap had protected his face from the rain, but now he was practically drowning in it.

"We're closed," the woman said.

Another woman appeared, saying, "What is it, Gertrude?" This one was shorter and wore a neck brace and looked irritable.

"He wanted coffee and Danish," Gertrude said. "I told him we were closed."

"We *are* closed," the other woman said.

"Well, we're police officers," the lieutenant started.

"I know," said Gertrude. "I could tell by your hat."

"And your car," said the other woman. "It says 'Police' on the side."

The lieutenant turned his head and looked at the patrol car, even though he already knew what it said on its side. He quickly looked back and said, "Well, we're on duty here, and we were wondering if you could maybe sell us some coffee and Danish even if you aren't one hundred percent open." He tried a winning smile, but all he got for it was a mouthful of rain.

"We don't have any Danish," the irritable woman in the neck brace said.

Gertrude, being more kindly, said, "I'd like to help you out, but the fact is, we don't have any electricity yet. Nothing's hooked up at all. We just got here. I'd like a cup of coffee myself."

"It's getting damn cold in here," said the irritable woman, "with that door open."

"Well, thanks anyway," said the lieutenant.

Gertrude said, "Come around when we're open. We'll give you coffee and Danish on the house."

"I'll do that," said the lieutenant and slogged back through the puddles to report, saying, "They don't have any electricity, Captain. They're not set up for anything yet."

"We can't even pick a hilltop right," the captain said. To the radio man he said, "You!"

"Sir?"

"Find out if there's any patrol cars around here."

"Yes, sir."

"We want coffees and Danish."

"Yes, sir. How do you like your coffee?"

"Light, three sugars."

The radio man looked ill. "Yes, sir. Lieutenant?"

"Black, one Sweet 'n Low."

"Yes, sir."

While the radio man took the driver's order, the captain turned to the lieutenant and said, "One sweet and what?"

"It's a sugar substitute, sir. For people on diets."

"You're on a diet."

"Yes, sir."

"I weigh about twice as much as you, Lieutenant, but *I'm* not on a diet."

The lieutenant opened his mouth, but once again no response seemed exactly right, and he didn't say anything.

But silence, this time, was also a mistake. The captain's brows beetled, and he said, "Just what do you mean by that, Lieutenant?"

The radio man said, "I put in the order, sir."

It was a timely distraction. The captain thanked him and subsided again and brooded out the window for the next ten minutes, until another patrol car arrived, delivering the coffee and Danish. The captain cheered up at that, until the second patrol car arrived two minutes after the first, bringing more coffee and Danish. "I should have guessed," the captain said.

When the third and fourth patrol cars with shipments of coffee and Danish arrived simultaneously, the captain roared at the radio man, "Tell them enough! Tell them to stop, tell them it's enough, tell them I'm near the breaking point!"

"Yes, sir," said the radio man and got to work on the phone.

Nevertheless, two more patrol cars arrived with coffee and Danish in the next five minutes. It was the captain's belief that discipline was best maintained by never letting the ranks know when things louse up, so they had to accept and pay for and say thank you for each and every shipment, and gradually the mobile headquarters was filling up with plastic cups of coffee and brown paper bags full of Danish. The smell of the lieutenant's wet uniform combined with the steam of diner coffee was becoming very strong and fogging up the windows.

The lieutenant pushed several wooden stirrers off his lap and said, "Captain, I have an idea."

"God protect me," said the captain.

"The people working in that diner don't have any electricity or heat, sir. Frankly, they strike me as born losers. Why don't we give them some of our extra coffee and Danish?"

The captain considered. "I suppose," he said judiciously, "it's better than me getting out of the car and stamping all this stuff into the gravel. Go ahead, Lieutenant."

"Thank you, sir."

The lieutenant gathered up one carton—four coffees, four Danish—and carried it from the car over to the diner. He knocked on the door, and it was opened immediately by Gertrude, who still had a cigarette stuck in the corner of her mouth. The lieutenant said, "We got more food delivered than we wanted. I thought maybe you could use some of—'"

"We sure could," Gertrude said. "That's really sweet of you."

The lieutenant handed up the carton. "If you need any more," he said, "we've got plenty."

Gertrude looked hesitant. "Well, uh . . ."

"Are there more than four of you? I mean it, we're loaded down with the stuff."

Gertrude seemed reluctant to say how many of them were in the diner—probably because she didn't want to strain the lieutenant's generosity. But finally she said, "There's, uh, there's seven of us."

"Seven! Wow, you must really be working in there."

"Oh, yes," she said. "We really are."

"You must be in a hurry to open up."

"We really want to open it up," Gertrude said, nodding, the cigarette waggling in the corner of her mouth. "You couldn't be more right about that."

"I'll get you some more," the lieutenant said. "Be right back."

"You're really very kind," she said.

The lieutenant went back to the patrol car and opened

the rear door. "They can use some more," he said and assembled two more cartons.

The captain gave him a cynical look. He said, "You're delivering coffee and Danish to a diner, Lieutenant."

"Yes, sir, I know."

"It doesn't strike you as strange?"

The lieutenant paused in his shuffling of coffee containers. "Sir," he said, "my basic feeling about this whole business is that I'm actually in a hospital somewhere, undergoing major surgery, and this day is a dream I'm having while under the anesthetic."

The captain looked interested. "I imagine that's a very comforting thought," he said.

"It is, sir."

"Hmmmmm," said the captain.

The lieutenant carried more coffee and Danish to the diner, and Gertrude met him at the door. "How much do we owe you?"

"Oh, forget it," the lieutenant said. "I'll take a free cheeseburger some time when you're doing business."

"If only all police officers were like you," Gertrude said, "the world would be a far better place."

The lieutenant had often thought the same thing himself. He gave a modest smile and scuffed his foot in a puddle and said, "Oh, well, I just try to do my best."

"I'm sure you do. Bless you."

The lieutenant carried his happy smile back to the patrol car, where he found the captain in a sour mood again, beetle-browed and grumpy. "Something go wrong, sir?"

"I tried that anesthetic thing of yours."

"You did, sir?"

"I keep worrying how the operation's going to come out."

"I make it appendicitis, sir. There's really no danger in that."

The captain shook his head. "It's just not my style, Lieutenant," he said. "I'm a man who faces reality."

"Yes, sir."

"And I tell you this, Lieutenant. This day will end. It

can't go on forever. This day will come to an end. Some day it will."

"Yes, sir."

Conversation lagged for a while after that. Even with the twelve coffees and Danish the Lieutenant had given away, there had still been three sets for each man in the mobile headquarters. They hadn't drunk all the coffee, but they'd eaten all the Danish and were now feeling somnolent and sluggish. The driver fell into a deep sleep, the captain napped, and the lieutenant kept dropping off and then waking up again with a start. The radio man never quite lost consciousness, though he did take his shoes off and rest his head against the window and hold his microphone slackly in his lap.

The morning passed slowly, with undiminished rain and no positive news in any of the infrequent crackling radio contacts from headquarters. Noontime came and went, and the afternoon began heavily to row past, and by two o'clock they were all feeling restless and cramped and irritable and uncomfortable. Their mouths tasted bad, their feet had swollen, their underwear chafed, and it had been hours since any of them had relieved themselves.

Finally, at ten past two, the captain grunted and shifted position and said, "Enough is enough."

The other three tried to look alert.

"We're not accomplishing anything out here," the captain said. "We're not mobile, we're not in contact with anybody, we're not getting anywhere. Driver, take us back to headquarters."

"Yes, sir!"

As the car started forward, the lieutenant looked out at the diner one last time and wondered if the thing would actually stay in business long enough for him to get that free cheeseburger. He was sorry for the people trying to run the place, but somehow he doubted it.

29

"THERE they go!" Victor shouted.

"At goddam last," said Murch's Mom and started at once undoing the straps on her neck brace.

Dortmunder had been sitting at the table with May, practicing holding his hands together as if he had the cuffs on. Now he cocked an eye toward Victor and said, "You sure they're leaving?"

"Gone," Victor said. "Absolutely gone. Made a U-turn out there by the sign and took off."

"And about time," May said. The floor around the chair where she was sitting was littered with tiny cigarette ends.

Dortmunder sighed. When he got to his feet his bones creaked; he felt old and stiff and achey all over. He shook his head, thought of adding a comment, and decided just to let it go.

The last four hours had been hell. And yet, when he and Kelp had first seen this spot, it had seemed like a special dispensation from Heaven. The big sign out by the road, the empty gravel parking lot, and a blank space where the diner should be; who could ask for anything more? They'd rushed back to the Wanderlust Trailer Park, where Murch already had the bank attached to the horse van, and quickly they'd brought the whole kit and caboodle over here, except for the stolen station wagon, which they'd left in somebody's driveway along the way. Victor and Kelp had gone a block or so ahead in the Packard, to watch out for cops, and Murch had followed with the horse van and the bank—his Mom and May riding with him in the cab of the van, Dortmunder and Herman back in the bank. They'd gotten here with no trouble, positioned the bank, parked the van and the Packard out of sight behind it, and gone back to business as usual, the only changes being that Herman had to use battery-operated power tools again and the hearts game had been resumed by flashlight. Also, the rainwater drenching down the metal skin of the bank quickly chilled the interior, and made everybody feel a little stiff and rheumatic. But it hadn't been terrible, and they'd mostly been in a pretty good mood—even Herman, who had regained his belief in his ability to get into any safe, if given sufficient time.

And then the cops had arrived. Kelp had seen them first, glancing out the window and saying, "Look! Law!"

The rest of them had crowded to the windows and stared out at the police car parked out by the sign. May had said, "What are they going to do? Are they onto us?"

"No." That had been Victor, always ready with an opinion based on his experiences with the other side of the law. "They're just on patrol," he'd said. "If they were interested in us, they'd handle the situation differently."

"Like surround the place," Dortmunder had suggested.

"Exactly."

Then the one cop had gotten out of the car and come over, and it had turned out their cover was working. Still, it was hard to concentrate with that damn police car ever-lastingly parked outside the bank you'd just stolen, and the hearts game had finally just dwindled away and stopped. Everybody had sat around, irritable and nervous, and every five minutes or so somebody would ask Victor, "What the hell are they doing out there?" Or "When are they going to go away, for the love of God?" And Victor would shake his head and say, "I just don't know. I'm baffled."

When the other police cars started showing up, one and two at a time, the whole crew inside the bank began to bounce around as agitated as kittens in a sack. "What are they *doing?*" everybody asked, and Victor kept saying, "I don't *know,* I don't *know.*"

It later turned out, of course, that the other cars had all been delivering orders of coffee and Danish. When Dortmunder had finally come to that understanding, he'd told the others and added, "Which means they're as loused up as we are. Which gives me hope."

Still, the time had passed slowly. The extra coffee and Danish they were given by the cops helped a lot—they were all getting pretty cold and hungry by then—but as the hours went by they all began to see themselves either starving or freezing to death, trapped in this stupid bank forever by a bunch of cops who didn't even know they were in the same county.

Also, Herman was restricted in the attacks he could make on the safe while the police car was parked out front. The grinding on the circular hole could continue, but things like explosions had to wait. This made Herman fretful, and he tended to pace back and forth from one end of the bank to the other and snarl at people.

Then there was the business of the neck brace. Murch carried on so much about it that his Mom finally agreed to wear it as long as the police car was out front, but she was disposed to be testy while her head was propped up by the thing, so that made two soreheads prowling around, which didn't help matters any.

And then, all at once, they left. No reason, no explanation, their departure as abrupt and senseless as their arrival, they up and went. And suddenly everybody was smiling, even Murch's Mom, who had flung the neck brace into the farthest corner of the bank.

"Now," Herman said. "Now I get to try what I've wanted to do for the last two hours. Longer. Since before noon."

Dortmunder was walking around in a figure eight, moving his shoulders and elbows, trying to loosen up. "What's that?" he said.

"That circular groove," Herman told him. "I think we've got it deep enough now, so if I pack the groove with plastic explosive, it just might pop it out of there."

"Then let's do it," Dortmunder said. "Before the Health Department comes around to inspect the kitchen and the bread man starts making deliveries, let's do it and get the hell out of here."

"This'll be a bigger explosion than before," Herman warned. "I want you to know that."

Dortmunder stopped figure-eighting. Voice flat, he said, "Will we survive it?"

"Oh, sure! Not *that* big!"

"That's all I ask," Dortmunder said. "My wants are simple."

"Take me about five minutes to set up," Herman said.

It took less. Four minutes later, Herman made everybody get around on the other side of the partition from the safe, explaining, "This might throw a little metal around."

"Good," Dortmunder said. "I feel like doing the same thing myself."

They all waited out in the main part of the bank while Herman, out of sight, did his final bit of work. After a few seconds of silence, they watched him back slowly into view around the end of the partition, holding a length of wire in each hand, gently drawing the wires after him. He looked at the others over his shoulder. "Everybody set?"

"Blow the damn thing," Dortmunder said.

"Right." Herman touched the exposed ends of wire together, and from the other side of the partition came a *Krack!* The bank rocked, much more than with the earlier explosions, and a stack of empty plastic coffee containers fell off the desk over in the corner where May had left them. "Got it," Herman said, smiling all over his face, and a bit of gray smoke came curling around the edge of the partition.

They all crowded around the partition to look at the safe, and damn if it didn't have a round hole in the side. Kelp shouted, "You did it!"

"God *damn!*" Herman cried, delighted with himself, and everybody pummeled him on the back.

Dortmunder said, "Why's the smoke coming out of there?"

They all got quiet again and looked at the wisp of smoke curling up from the hole. Herman said, "Wait a minute now," and stepped forward to take a quick look around on the floor. Then he turned to Dortmunder, outraged, and said, "You know what happened?"

"No," Dortmunder said.

"The goddam metal fell *inside,*" Herman said.

Kelp had gone over to look in the hole, and now he said, "Hey. The money's on fire."

That caused general panic, but Dortmunder pushed his way through the mob and took a look inside, and it wasn't as bad as all that. The hole in the side of the safe was perfectly round and about a foot in diameter, and inside there was a round piece of black metal the same size, like a midget manhole cover except much thicker, and it was resting on stacks of money, and it was setting them on fire. Not very much, just browning and curling them around the edge of the circle. However, a couple of little flames had already puffed into life, and if left to themselves they would spread and eventually all of the money would turn into ashes.

"Okay," Dortmunder said, partly to calm the people behind him, partly to challenge the fates. He took off his right shoe, stuck it in through the hole and began to slap the fire out.

"If only we had water," Victor said.

Murch's Mom said, "The toilet tank! We haven't flushed since we left the trailer park, the tank should still be full!"

That had been another problem, four hours stuck in here without toilet facilities, but now this one too turned out to be a blessing in disguise. A coffee-container brigade was set up, and pretty soon Dortmunder could put his shoe back on and pour water on the smoldering bills instead. It took only four containers, and the last ember was out.

"Wet money," Dortmunder grumbled and shook his head. "All right, where's the plastic bags?"

They'd brought along a box of plastic garbage-can liner bags to carry the money in. May got them now, pulled one out of the box, and Dortmunder and Kelp started filling it with charred bills, wet bills and good bills while May and Victor held the bag open.

And then Murch's Mom shouted, "We're moving!"

Dortmunder straightened, his hands full of money. "What?"

Murch came running around the partition, looking much more agitated than Dortmunder had ever seen him. "We're rolling," he said. "We're rolling down the goddam hill, and we're out of control!"

30

KELP pushed the door open and watched countryside going by. "We're going out on the road!"

Behind him, Herman shouted, "Jump! Jump!"

How fast were they going? Probably no more than five or ten miles an hour, but to Kelp's eyes the pavement going by beneath his feet was just a blur.

But they had to jump. There were no windows in the front of the bank, so they couldn't see where they were headed, whether they were going to crash into something or not. They weren't going very fast yet because the slope wasn't at all steep here, but the bank was angling toward the road, and down a ways farther the hill did get a lot steeper, and then they'd go too fast to jump. So it had to be now, and at this door Kelp was first.

He jumped. Off to his right, uphill, he was aware of Victor jumping from the other door. Then Kelp hit the pavement, lost his footing, sprawled and rolled over twice. When he sat up, he had a new big tear in his right trouser knee, and the rest of the gang was spread out downhill, all sitting and lying on the pavement in the rain, with the bank rolling on away from them, on the road now and picking up speed.

Kelp looked the other way, to see how Victor was doing, and Victor was on his feet already and hobbling back toward the diner site. Kelp couldn't figure that out for a second, and then he realized Victor was going after the Packard. To give chase, to get the bank back!

Kelp got to his feet and limped off in Victor's wake, but hadn't even reached the gravel driveway yet when the Packard came tearing up and squealed to a stop beside him. He climbed in, and Victor gunned the motor again. He was going to stop for Dortmunder, who was next, standing there with the plastic bag full of money in his hand, but Dortmunder urgently waved them on, and Kelp said, "Don't stop, Victor, they'll come along in the van."

"Okay," Victor said and tromped on the accelerator.

The bank was far away down the long slope. It was rainy, it was mid-afternoon, and they were far out on Long Island, three things that helped to give them an empty road when they needed it. The bank, whizzing down the exact middle of the two-lane road, straddling the white line, happily met no traffic coming the other way.

"It's gonna go over at the curve," Kelp said. "It'll crash down there, but we should have time to get the rest of the money out."

But it didn't go over. The curve was banked, angled properly, and the bank rolled around it with no trouble at all—around and out of sight.

"God *damn* it!" yelled Kelp. "Catch up with it, Victor."

"I will," Victor said. Hunched over the wheel, his attention fixed on the road ahead, he said, "You know what I think happened?"

"The bank started to roll," Kelp said.

"Because of the explosion," Victor said. "That's what I think did it. You felt the way that made it rock. It must have started it, and we were on top of a hill, and once it was moving it just kept going."

"It sure did," Kelp said. He shook his head. "You can't believe how irritated Dortmunder is going to be," he said.

Victor snapped a glance at the rear-view mirror. "Not behind us yet," he said.

"They'll be along. Let's worry about the bank first."

They reached the curve, spun around it, and saw the bank well out in front. There was a small town at the base of the hill, a little fishing community, and the bank was headed straight for it.

But Victor was gaining. Also, as the road leveled out at the bottom, the bank began slowly to lose its momentum. When it ran the red light in the center of town it wasn't doing any more than twenty-five miles an hour. A woman crossing guard blew her whistle at the bank as it went through the light, but it didn't stop. Victor slowed, seeing the woman in her policelike uniform and white crossing-guard belt, and seeing the red light, but as he reached the intersection the light turned green and he accelerated again. The woman had whistled herself breathless, and as they went by she was standing in the rainy gutter, panting, her shoulders heaving, her mouth open.

"It'll stop soon," Kelp said hopefully. "There isn't any slope here at all."

"That's the ocean," Victor said, nodding ahead.

"Oh, no!"

The end of the street was a pier, jutting out a good thirty feet into the water. Victor caught up with the bank just before it trundled out onto the pier, but it didn't matter; there was no way of stopping it. One fisherman in yellow rubber slicker and rain hat, sitting on a folding chair, looked up and saw the bank coming and leaped straight from his chair into the ocean; the bank, *en passant*, flipped his chair after him. He had been the only occupant of the pier, which now the bank had to itself.

"Make it stop!" Kelp cried as Victor slammed the Packard to a halt at the beginning of the pier. "We've got to make it stop!"

"No way," Victor said. "There's just no way."

The two of them sat in the Packard and watched the bank roll inexorably out along the rumbling boards of the pier to the very end and quietly, undramatically, roll off the outer edge and drop like a stone into the water.

Kelp groaned.

"One thing," Victor said. "It was beautiful to watch."

"Victor," Kelp said. "Do me one favor. Don't say that to Dortmunder."

Victor looked at him. "No?"

"He wouldn't understand," Kelp said.

"Oh." Victor looked out the windshield again. "I wonder how deep it is out there," he said.

"Why?"

"Well, maybe we could swim down to it and get the rest of the money."

Kelp gave him a pleased smile. "You're right," he said. "If not today, maybe sometime when the sun's shining."

"And it's warmer."

"Right."

"Unless," Victor said, "someone else sees it there and reports it."

"Say," Kelp said, frowning out the windshield again. "There was somebody on the pier."

"There was?"

"A fisherman, in a yellow raincoat."

"I didn't see him."

"We better take a look."

The two of them got out of the car and walked through the rain out onto the pier. Kelp looked over the edge and saw the man in the yellow raincoat climbing up the scaffolding along the side. "Let me give you a hand," he called and knelt to reach down to him.

The fisherman looked up. His face looked astonished. He said, "You won't believe what happened. I don't believe it myself."

Kelp helped him up onto the pier. "We saw it go," he said. "A runaway trailer."

"It just come right along," the fisherman said, "and threw me in the ocean. Lost my chair, lost my tackle, damn near lost myself."

"You kept your hat anyway," Victor pointed out.

"Tied under my chin," the fisherman said. "Was there anybody in that thing?"

"No, it was empty," Kelp said.

The fisherman looked down at himself. "My wife told me," he said. "She said this wasn't no day to fish. I'll be goddamned if she wasn't right for once."

"Just so you didn't get hurt," Kelp said.

"Hurt?" The fisherman grinned. "Listen," he said. "I come out of this with the kind of fish story you just can't top. I wouldn't care if I got a broken leg out of it."

"You didn't, did you?" Victor asked.

The fisherman stomped his booted feet on the planks of the pier; they squished. "Hell, no," he said. "Fit as a fiddle." He sneezed. "Except I do believe I'm coming down with pneumonia."

"Maybe you ought to get home," Kelp said. "Get into some dry things."

"Bourbon," the fisherman said. "That's what I need." He glanced away toward the end of the pier. "Damnedest thing I ever saw," he said and sneezed again and went off shaking his head.

"Let's take a look," Kelp said. He and Victor walked out to the end of the pier and stared down into the rain-spattered water. "I don't see it," Kelp said.

"Here it is. See it?"

Kelp looked where Victor was pointing. "Right," he said, catching a glimpse of the thing, like a blue-and-white whale down there in the water. Then he frowned, peering at it, and said, "Hey, it's moving."

"It is?"

The two of them squinted in silence for ten seconds or so, and then Victor said, "You're right. It's the undertow, taking it away."

"I don't believe it," Kelp said.

Victor looked back toward shore. "Here comes the rest of them," he said.

Kelp reluctantly turned and saw the other five getting out of the horse van. They came trailing out onto the pier, Dortmunder in the lead. Kelp put a sickly smile on his face and waited.

Dortmunder came up and looked into the water. "I don't suppose you two are out here for a tan," he said.

"No," said Kelp.

Dortmunder nodded at the water. "It went in there, right?"

"That's right," Kelp said. "You can see it . . ." He pointed, then frowned. "No, you can't any more."

Victor said, "It's moving."

"Moving," Dortmunder echoed.

"Coming down the hill," Victor said, "the wind shut the doors again. I don't suppose it's completely airtight, but it is closed up pretty good, and it must have just enough air in it to make it buoyant enough not to be stuck in the mud or the sand on the bottom. So the undertow's moving it."

The others had come up by now. May said, "You mean it's going away?"

"That's right," Victor said.

Kelp felt Dortmunder looking at him but wouldn't acknowledge it. He kept staring into the water instead.

Murch's Mom said, "Where's it going to?"

"France," Dortmunder said.

Herman said, "You mean it's gone for good? After all that work?"

"Well, we got some of the money anyway," Kelp said and looked around with the sickly smile on his face again. But Dortmunder was already walking away along the pier toward the shore. One by one, the others followed him, and the rain rained down all around.

31

"TWENTY-THREE thousand, eight hundred twenty dollars," Dortmunder said and sneezed.

They were all in the apartment, his and May's. Everybody had changed clothes, with May and Murch's Mom both in clothing belonging to May, and all five men in Dortmunder's clothes. They were also all sneezing, and May had brewed up a lot of tea with whiskey in it.

"Twenty-three, almost twenty-four thousand," Kelp said brightly. "It could have been worse."

"Yes," Dortmunder said. "It could have been Confederate money."

Murch sneezed and said, "How much is that apiece?"

Dortmunder said, "First we pay off the financier. That's eight thousand, leaving fifteen thousand, eight hundred twenty. Divided by seven, that's two thousand, two hundred sixty bucks apiece."

Murch made a face as though something smelled bad. "Two thousand dollars? That's all?"

Herman and Murch's Mom sneezed simultaneously.

"We'll spend more than that in medical bills," Dortmunder said.

Victor said, "Still, we did the job, you have to admit that. You can't call it a failure."

"I can if I want to," Dortmunder said.

"Have some more tea," said May.

Kelp sneezed.

"Two thousand dollars," Herman said, and blew his nose. "I spill that much."

They were all in the living room, sitting around the money, the charred bills and wet bills and good bills all stacked in different piles on the coffee table. The apartment was warm and dry, but the smell of wet clothes and disaster filled the air from the bedroom.

Murch's Mom sighed. "I'll have to start wearing that brace again," she said.

"You lost it," her son told her accusingly. "You left it in the bank."

"So we'll buy a new one."

"Another expense."

"Well," Kelp said, "I guess we might as well divvy the loot and go on home."

"Divvy the loot," Dortmunder echoed and looked at the paper on the coffee table. "You got an eye dropper?"

"It isn't that bad," Kelp said. "We didn't come out of it empty-handed."

Victor got to his feet and stretched and said, "I suppose this would be more like a celebration if we'd gotten the rest of the money."

Dortmunder nodded. "You could say that."

They split up the cash and departed, everybody promising to send back the borrowed clothes and reclaim their own. Left to themselves, Dortmunder and May sat on the sofa and looked at the four thousand, five hundred twenty dollars left on the coffee table. They sighed. Dortmunder said, "Well, it did give me something to think about, I have to admit it."

"The worst thing about a cold," May said, "is the way it makes the cigarettes taste." She plucked the ember from the corner of her mouth and flipped it into an ashtray but didn't light a new one. "You want some more tea?"

"I still got some," He sipped at the tea and frowned. "What's the percentage of tea and whiskey in this thing?"

"About half and half."

He drank a little more. The warm steam curled around his nostrils. "You better brew up another pot," he said.

She nodded, starting to smile. "Right," she said.

32

"IT'S on the Island," Captain Deemer said. "It's some-where on this goddam Island."

"Yes, sir," Lieutenant Hepplewhite said, but faintly.

"And I'm going to find it."

"Yes, sir."

The two of them were alone in the unmarked patrol car, a black Ford, radio-equipped. The captain was driving, and the lieutenant was beside him. The captain hunched over the wheel, his eyes constantly moving as he drove back and forth and up and down and all over Long Island.

Beside him, the lieutenant's eyes were unfocused. He wasn't looking for or at anything, but was practicing once more the speech that he would never make to the captain. In its latest form it went: "Captain, it's been three weeks. You're letting the precinct go to hell, you've become ob-sessed with this missing bank, all you do is spend all the daylight hours, seven days a week, driving around looking for that bank. It's *gone,* Captain, that bank is gone and we are never going to find it.

"But, Captain, even if you are obsessed and can't get out of your obsession, *I'm not.* You pulled me off night duty, and I loved night duty, I loved being the man behind the desk at night in the precinct. But you put that idiot Schlumgard in there in my place, and Schlumgard doesn't know what the hell he's doing, and morale is going to hell. If I ever *do* get my job back, Schlumgard will have undone everything I've tried to do.

"But the point is, Captain, it has been *three weeks.* The

New York City police stopped cooperating after four days, which means the bank could have been taken out of our jurisdiction anytime in the last two and a half weeks, which means it could be anywhere in the world by now. I know your theory, Captain, that the bank was hidden sometime that first night, that the crooks emptied the safe in the first day or two and went away and just left it there, but even if you're right, what good does it do? If they hid it so well we couldn't find it in the first few days, when we had search parties combing the entire Island, two of us are not going to find it by driving around in a car three weeks later.

"Which is why, Captain, I feel I must tell you that I have come to a decision. If you want to go on looking for the bank, that's up to you. But either you let me go back to my regular duties, or I'll just have to talk to the Commissioner. Now, Captain, I've gone along with you on every—"

"You say something?"

Startled, the lieutenant snapped his head around and stared at the captain. "What? What?"

Captain Deemer frowned at him, then faced the road again. "I thought you said something."

"No, sir."

"Well, just keep your eyes open."

"Yes, sir."

The lieutenant looked out the side window, though without any hope. They were climbing a hill, and just ahead was the sign for McKay's Diner. The lieutenant remembered the free cheeseburger he'd been promised, and smiled. He was about to turn his head toward the captain and suggest they stop for a snack when he saw the diner was gone again. "Well, I'll be darned," he said.

"What?"

"That diner, sir," the lieutenant said as they drove by. "They went out of business already."

"Is that right." The captain didn't sound interested.

"Even faster than I thought," the lieutenant said, looking back at the space where the diner had been.

"We're looking for a bank, Lieutenant, not a diner."

"Yes, sir." The lieutenant faced front, began again to scan the countryside. "I knew they wouldn't make it," he said.